Glitter Magic Fairies

Joe

Table of Contents

For anyone who has ever been bullied

You're not alone!!

The Author wishes to give a big thanks to Leisa for believing in me,
and your hours spent deciphering my ramblings.

ISBN 978-0-6453423-5-2

Also available in E-Book ISBN 978-0-6453423-4-5

Joe

Chapter 1

I can faintly hear a phone ringing in my sleep, for a minute I'm not sure if it's just a part of my dream. I sit up and look at the clock and it's 2:30 am. The phone is still ringing. I can hear my grandma shuffling from the spare room where she has been staying, to answer it. I climb out of my bed and go out to the hallway. I am rubbing the sleep from my eyes, so I can see where I am walking. I wish to inquire who is ringing at this hour of the morning, disturbing the household and waking everyone up. I see my grandma drop the phone, and fall to the floor, no no she says over and over again. I walk over to her and crouch beside her, she pulls me into her. She holds me tight. The phone is still hanging near the floor. I can faintly hear a voice on the other end saying, "Hello, are you there?" several times.

Then I hear the beep beep beep to signal the other person had hung up. We sit there on the floor, with her crying and me not having a clue why, for about thirty minutes, then there is a knock on the door. I go to answer it and my Aunty Denny is standing there, her eyes red and blotchy. She reaches down and ruffles my hair. She tells me to go and put a warm jacket and my runners on. She headed to the phone table and picked the hanging phone up and put it back in its cradle. Then she helped my grandma up off the floor and told her to go get cleaned up, we had to get going.

Going where I wondered? Surely it was too early to be going anywhere. It was still dark outside, not early in the morning before the sun comes up dark, but middle of the night, when the monsters come out from under beds dark. I hoped where ever we were going we would be back in time for me to tend to my horses. If I didn't get my chores done before school my dad would lecture me about neglecting my responsibilities, and depending on what mood he was in, I would either be grounded, or get a belting. I put the things on I was asked to, then went and stood in the hall way, I wasn't sure what else to do. Soon I was joined by my aunt, she knelt down in front of me and told me there had been an accident, the big white 4x4 that was towing the horse float, had hit a patch of ice on the road. I blinked at her not fully understanding what she was saying. Dad had a big white 4x4, him and mum and my big brother were in northern New South Wales, at a horse stud, picking up a new pony for my brother, he had out grown the old one, and she was now mine.

My aunt hugged me and told me we had to go to get to the hospital. They had all been air lifted to Brisbane. As it was the closest major hospital to where the accident had occurred. I nodded, but still had no clue what she was talking about. Grandma came out of the room she had been staying in. She grabbed my hand and we headed to the car. We lived about half way between Brisbane and the Gold Coast in the hinterland. On a huge horse stud. Brisbane was about two hours away. I slept in the car all the way to the hospital. I remember my aunt picking me up from the back seat and carrying me into the hospital, this would be the first of many times I was to see the inside of that hospital. She was rushing, and grandma was having trouble keeping up with her. We were pointed to the emergency department. When we got there my aunt stood me up on the ground. I looked around at my surroundings, we were in a room that was like a big hallway, with white hospital beds on either side. I looked up at the bed in front of me, my dad was laying there, a tube going into his nose, white sticking plasters patches on his head, he did not have a shirt on and there were ugly red bleeding blotches over his chest, and tummy. He had a bandage wrapped around his right shoulder crossed over to his left ribs. Daddy, I cried out. My aunt lifted me up and daddy used his good hand to stroke my hair. He told me he was ok, just battered and bruised. Where was my mum I demanded? I saw my dad look at my aunt, and grandma started crying again. Your mum is having an operation dad told me.

"Where is Kevin?" I asked next.

My dad's eyes filled with tears, and he shook his head, "Kevin is having an operation too," he said.

A nurse in a stiff white uniform came to dads' bed, and pushed us out of the way, she stuck a thermometer in dads' mouth, and put a black belt around his arm, then pumped it up with a little black thing in her hand. I heard dad ask the nurse if there was any word yet. She had a sad look on her face and shook her head. We stayed at the hospital for ages, I curled up on dads' bed with him, and went to sleep. When I woke up, the sun was shining through the curtains at the other end of the room. Someone brought in a breakfast tray, and dad let me have the toast and the apple juice. Gran and my aunt left the room to go and get a coffee. As I was eating the toast a doctor came up to dad's bed. He asked how dad was feeling, and said he could go home later today, his injuries were mostly superficial whatever that meant.

When I finished the toast, before my aunt and grandmother returned, dad said we were going for a little walk. We walked out of the room to an elevator and on the elevator dad pushed the button two floors up from where we currently were. He picked me up with his good arm, and carried me the rest of the way, snuggling his head into the side of my neck, I could feel his tears hitting my shoulder. I still really did not understand what was going on. We entered a hall-way, this one was filled with ladies in beds. We walked down the row of beds and stopped at the middle bed. The bed had the curtains pulled around it. Dad pulled the curtains back and we went into the room. I did not recognise the person lying in the bed, their head was bandaged up and all around the eyes was black. There was dried blood on a swollen chin, and the bottom half of one lip was completely missing. One arm was covered in hard plaster and it was being held up in the air by a chain and a leg was being held up the same way. All that was visible was the toes, the rest of the leg right up to the bum was in hard white plaster. Dad sat me in the chair beside the bed. He walked around to the arm that wasn't in plaster, and picked up the hand

and kissed it. I heard him explaining to the figure on the bed between his sobs that 'he' was still in surgery. The figure in the bed started to cry.

Dad tried to comfort them. We stayed in that room for ages, Grandma and my aunt found us there. They were all crying, and even though I didn't know why, it made me sad as well.

We were all still in there when a different doctor came in, he was checking on the figure in the bed. As he was checking, he said Wendy. Instantly my ears pricked up, Wendy was my mummies name. Was that person on the bed my mummy? It did not look anything like her. I was sitting very quietly and very still on the bottom of the bed. But I had to find out if it was my mummy, so I called out Mummy, the head moved, and the figure tried to speak, but was unable to make any sounds I could understand. "Yes," grandma explained to me, "That's your mummy."

 I started to cry lots then. "Mummy, Mummy what's happened to you?" I wailed.

I was starting to get a little carried away. And I was just about to have a full tantrum, I wanted my mummy. My aunt picked me up and carried me outside to see the trees. She sat me on a chair, and explained to me again, that mummy, daddy and Kevin had been in a car accident, daddy was ok, and mummy would be ok, but right now she was very sore, as she had broken bones.

I kind of knew what broken bones felt like, I had broken my arm last year, from falling off my pony.

"What about Kevin?" I asked my bottom lip trembling. "Where is Kevin? I have not seen him yet."

My aunt told me Kevin was still being operated on, and the doctors were doing what they could.

"Is he going to be ok?" I enquired.

"We don't know yet," was all she said.

"What about the pony, they were picking up for Kevin?" I asked.

"The pony is ok and will be waiting at home for your brother when he gets better. Now if you promise me you're going to be good, we can go back inside to your mum and dad." she said.

"I'll be good," I promised through my sobs.

That's one of my earliest childhood memories. I was five, nearly six. From that day on, nothing was ever the same.

Chapter 2

I was eight now, but the horror of that night never left me. Mum had come home from hospital about four weeks later, she would always walk with a limp, and her arm would never be as good as it used to be. But she had changed as well, she no longer picked me up and hugged me, or spent time with me. If I asked her a question, she would brush me away, or she herself would just walk away from me. No longer did we all eat as a family at the table, mum preferred to eat in front of the television, and dad took his food either to the stables or to his office. Sometimes it was just me sitting alone at the dining table, with grandma bustling around in the kitchen.

We spent hours at the hospital with Kevin. The doctors said when he was thrown from the car, he broke bones in his back, and severely injured his spinal column. I did not know exactly what that meant then. He almost had to have his leg below the knee amputated, because he got an infection in it, and the doctors could not stop the infection from spreading. Dad pleaded with them to try something different and just give his leg an extra week, he even hired a nurse to sit at the hospital beside Kevin and massage his leg day and night. It worked, and the leg was saved. He also suffered major brain damage from hitting big rocks when he was thrown out of the car. They had tried over twenty surgeries to make it right, but in the end, there was nothing else they could do. The doctors said he would be a quadriplegic for the rest of his life. He would need specialist round the clock nursing, and physiotherapy, his life expectancy was less than five years. Kevin spent eighteen months in the hospital. He was in a wheel chair, and would be for the rest of his life. He was unable to do anything for himself. Mum and dad tried to do it all on their own for about six months, but it was too much, and they ended up hiring a nurse.

Grandma was living with us permanently now, well not in our house, she said that was crowded enough. But she got my uncle to build her a little cottage, right on top of the small mountain, that over looked our property. A little creek separated her from us, and she had a little bridge built over it. There was no electricity in the cottage, because that's the way grandma wanted it. She had a fire stove, which kept the house snug and warm in winter, but was way too hot in summer. There was only one room in the cottage, but she had a curtain put up so she could sleep in private she said. I had a lot of responsibilities now including looking after the riding ponies. We ran a horse stud, we bred and sold quarter horses. The best all round type of horse, well that's what dad always said anyway. Mostly we sold colts and fillies, unbroken or raw as dad called them.

Sometimes one wouldn't sell, and dad and us boys would help break it in, then he would sell it a year or so later as a kid's pony. By the time they finished putting up with us, dad reckoned they would be bomb proof.

As Kevin could no longer help with the horses at all, and dad just did not have the time anymore, the breaking in of the unsold colts and fillies became my sole responsibility. As was riding my own little pony, and Kevin's new pony that he never even got to ride. I also had other chores, like feeding all the riding horses and ponies, cleaning their stalls, gathering and bagging the horse poo from the yards, and putting it at the front of our property for sale. It was great for the garden and people couldn't get enough of it. The only advantage to that was, for every Two-dollar bag I sold, I got to keep One dollar and fifty cents of the money. The other fifty cents was a 'corporate' fee, and went straight to the jar in Dads study. I was saving most of the money, I did not really want or need anything. I was just saving it for a rainy day.

Even with a nurse, Kevin still took up most of my parents' time. Mum had to leave her full-time job as a dance instructor, she said she wasn't able to do it anymore anyway, because of her leg. Sometimes if I was in the back yard I would see her through the windows in her studio, stretching, or sitting on the floor crying. Dad spent all day with the horses, but then at night had to help mum with Kevin. The nurse did not live in, and left at 5pm every day, and she didn't work on week-ends. While she was here mum had to try to run around and do whatever else needed doing. Grandma came down from her cottage at 7am every morning, to help get me off to school, do the house work, and be an extra set of hands if the nurse needed them, while mum was out, dropping me at school and doing the other things that needed to be done. Grandma also prepared and usually cooked our evening meal.

She made sure I was bathed, and cleaned, and helped me with my homework. I loved having her close to us.

But I missed my brother terribly, yes, he was still here, but he wasn't able to run with me, we couldn't ride our horses together anymore. We used to have play fights, and swim in the creek, and go on camp outs on the property. He taught me how to put a worm on a hook, and fish. He loved magic, and he had a magic kit bought for him for one of his birthdays. The kit contained all sorts of magic tricks, disappearing coins, and balls that vanished before your eyes, flowers and ribbons that appeared out of nowhere. He had also learnt a few card tricks, every so often he would learn a new magic trick, and we would be made to sit in the lounge and watch him perform. He had a black magicians cape, with lots of secret pockets in it. I was only little then and I remember being astonished and amazed at the great Kevinni and his travelling magic show.

Mum and dad forbade me from seeing him now, they said it would upset me too much. I think I was more upset at NOT seeing him.

While grandma was here and great to have around, sometimes she was too busy helping with Kevin, or she was sick and couldn't be here for a days at a time. Sometimes the creek would flood and she wouldn't be able to get here. These times are the times when I had to fend for myself. I learnt the hard way, about most things, for example burnt toast can cause the kitchen curtains to catch fire. I was seven when that happened dad belted me so hard I could not stand up for a week. He told me it was time I grew up, because him and mum did not have the time for me to still be a babied little boy. I was going to be the man of this family someday, and its time I started to take some responsibility around the farm.

That was my wake-up call and from that day on I never asked anyone for anything, including help. I learnt to do things on my own, I never gave up, if there was something I couldn't do I kept at it until I could do it. I also learnt to be ok with just my own company, as much as any seven-year-old could. I learnt to tie my own shoes, make myself a fried egg and toast, brush my own hair, and so much more. Mum however refused to teach me how to do my own washing, I was allowed to take my clothes to the laundry, but then I had to leave them in the basket with my name on it. The washing machine was brand new, and mum wouldn't let anyone else touch it.

Now I was able to lunge the big stallions and mares to give them exercise. I could even help a mare bring a foal into this world.

I still let grandma help me with stuff, not because I couldn't do it, but because I didn't want her to think she wasn't needed, and to leave us. She was still my favourite story teller. Sure, I could read myself, but why, it's better to be read to I think.

Mum and dad had started arguing, apparently the nurse fancied dad, and tried her hardest to get his attention, and this caused huge arguments. I learnt that when they were arguing I could sneak into my brother's room without being noticed. Dad had three rooms of the house modified, and they resembled a hospital room, everywhere was starched white linen, on the bed, the curtains, the nurse's uniforms and Kevin's pyjamas. There was a large white bathroom, the shower and bath tub were huge. There was an area where Kevin could sit in his wheel chair and watch a large television screen, or wheel up to a desk with a table, that had been made so as Kevin could be wheel up to it, and an under an overhanging bench made it seem as though he was just seated at a normal table. This is where he usually had his food. The nurse would sit on the other side of the table and feed him. No one was sure if the television helped or not, but his physician told us it wouldn't hurt him. When my parents argued, I would get to spend quite a bit of time with my brother. The arguments would always end with dad storming off to the stables, and mum driving away in her car, spinning the tyres and throwing up gravel and dust, spooking the paddocked horses, the whole way along the driveway.

I would sneak into his part of the house, with his magic set tucked under my arm, or his cards. I would perform magic tricks for him even though I was nowhere near as good as he used to be. I know my parents said he wasn't capable of anything, and he apparently could not recognise anyone, or show emotion of any kind. I swear that when I saw him his eyes would light up, and once when I had performed magic for him, I am positive I saw a tear fall from his eye. Sometimes I would just sit with him and read, while holding his hand in mine. Other times when I did not see the argument coming and I was unprepared I would just sit and talk to him, about everything, the farm, mum, dad, and the horses. Sometimes the nurse would see me with Kevin, but she never said anything, she would wink at me and go about doing whatever it was she was doing.

Just before my ninth birthday dad fired the nurse. Apparently, mum caught dad kissing her. Our house became a war zone from then on.

Chapter 3

For my tenth birthday, dad brought me my own Arabian colt, he wanted to introduce some height and more speed into some of our quarter horses. He was the most beautiful horse I had ever seen, he stood at approximately 20 hands high, he was dark dappled grey, and I guessed the older he got the lighter his colour would become. His mane and tail were grey and black streaked. Dad had him shipped up from the blue mountains, from an Arabian stud, it was winter so his coat was thick, soft and woolly.

He was only a couple years old and still had some growing to do. I would spend hours watching him. I was working him and trying to break him in, every time he got on the lunge lead and cantered, he would lift his head and his tail in the air, like he was showing off. I must admit I spent a lot more hours with him, sometimes working him, sometimes just sitting in his paddock watching him, he did not have a nasty bone in his body, and he loved nothing better than to kneel behind me and nuzzle his face into my hair. I brought him a big ball from a horse show I went to with dad. The ball was taller than I was. He would spend ages everyday kicking it and throwing it around his pen, some afternoons, I would play soccer with him, he seemed to have grasped the concept of kick and return really well. Although sometimes he would catch it in his teeth, and run around his pen at top speed with it firmly lodged in his mouth. I would end up falling into the dirt, from laughing so hard at him.

My brother had just turned fourteen. He had been surprising everyone with his progress the last twelve months, he could now focus his eyes, and blink in response to questions, He also had very slight movement in his hands, mainly his fingers. And he was trying to make sounds, and form words. Even the doctors couldn't believe it. Dad had hired a new male nurse a few months ago, he worked week-ends and started early. My brother hated him. I was spending a lot more time with my brother now, the doctor seemed to think I was responsible for the improvement in his health. Sometimes I would be sitting in his room with him, reading to him, we were currently reading the series about a boy wizard and were half way through the second book. When his nurse would arrive on his motor bike to start his shift. My brother would start thrashing around in his chair, and I am sure I had heard him rasp out the word no, a couple of times. No one could explain why my brother hated the nurse so much, the doctors said it was because the nurse, had to manipulate his muscles, and move all his joints and massage his arms and legs hands and feet, and this might be causing my brother discomfort. Nobody bothered to check him over, or look under his clothes.

But I had a feeling for a few weeks now that there was more to it. Although try as I might I was unable to prove it. I would barge into the room unexpectantly, trying to catch the nurse causing him discomfort, or make excuses to be in the room at weird times, but alas I came up empty handed every time.

My mum and dad had been arguing worse than ever, and mum had shouted at dad a couple of times, that life would have been easier if Kevin had of just died. I guess it was stressful on her, and I know sometimes her own pain consumed her. She blamed dad for the accident and for her no longer being able to dance. In lots of arguments in the past she had told him he had been driving way to fast. He always answered with, it was her who wanted to get home, he wanted to stay at a motel and head home the next day.

They were both missing the point it had been an 'accident' and no one's fault, sometimes bad stuff just happened. It was no one's fault.

Grandma started spending less time at our house. Most afternoons, after school I would take my homework up the steep path, and sit in her little cottage and do it, trying hard to ignore the screaming arguments coming from the house. I could see grandma was sick, but when I asked her about it, she told me she was ok, she just couldn't stand the arguing anymore.

Dad was her son, and the way mum was treating him was shameful. Grandma told me that when a relationship had deteriorated as much as this one had, then it was time to call it quits, for everyone's sake.

One afternoon Grandma told me she was going to go and stay with my uncle for a while, my dad's brother lived at Northgate, and had his own house building business. There was no reason for her to ever come back here.

 The first day she left, and I came home from school, I headed up to her cottage to see her. I sat at her table and cried my eyes out. I missed her like crazy.

Chapter 4

My twelfth birthday had been and gone months ago. Grandma still hadn't returned from my uncles. My parents now slept in separate bed rooms. My Arabian stallion's first foal was only weeks away from making its entrance into the world. Every morning I raced to the mare's stall. She was a chocolate brown doe-eyed, seven-year-old quarter horse, born and bred on our property, and possibly the last horse dad, Kevin and I had broken in together. I think that was why she was still here. I loved this mare almost as much as I loved my stallion. She had already had three foals, all healthy, no problems.

Kevin was still showing signs of improvement, although I knew he would never be able to leave the wheel chair. The male motorbike riding nurse was still here, as no one could find any obvious reason to fire him.

For the last few weeks, I had a strange tingling in my hands. I thought I may have pulled a muscle lunging one of the mares. People think stallions are bad, Broody mares are nastier than any stallion I have ever met. Last week I had one try and kill me through a fenced yard as I was walking past.

My eyes were changing too, every time I looked in a mirror, the shape had changed a little bit more. My irises were now long and pointed on both ends, and depending on how far away I was trying to look, depended on which way the pupil was. If I was looking at something in the distance, they were vertical, if I was focusing on something close, or reading, they sat vertically on my eye ball. They were changing colour daily too. Gone was the hazel green, I was born with, at present the colour was a dirty rusty brown, with mustard yellow closer to the pupil, the outside edge of my eyes was ice blue, and each day the ice blue colour was spreading, filling over the brown and yellow, and more over the iris. It was like the colours were raging their own private war in my eyes, and the blue was winning. I had never seen eyes like it on a human, I know cats have a pointed iris. But mine were truly a sight to be seen. Very cool!

About the time the tingling started, I started having weird dreams. I dreamt of Fairies, the real kind, with wings and magic. Puberty? Don't even go there, I blushed to the tips of my toes just hearing that word. The main fairy I dreamt of was almost two-hundred years old. Occasionally I could hear her speak to me when I wasn't asleep dreaming. She would tell me things, like I was destined to be amazing and that my time was coming, from now I would start to notice small changes about myself. She said my eye colour may change, and I would start to be able to feel some pains experienced by younger children, that I walked past or was near. My body would start to develop, way beyond anything puberty could throw at me. She also said I would never get pimples, or lankiness, greasy hair or most other ailments associated with teenagers.

She cautioned me to be careful around girls. She also told me the dreams were going to get more vivid, and that if I ever needed her for any reason all I had to do was call for her. She told me her name was Andy.

Some of the dreams I had were pretty messed up, fairies and little kids being bullied, pushed around, and worse. And flying, I had lots of dreams about flying, not in a plane, but with my very own wings.

About this time, I became the proud owner of a grey speckled chestnut filly, the grey was in swirls, almost complete circles, but not quite. She also had several, actual, dark purple strands in her mane and tail. I called her Molly. She was as unique as she was beautiful, dad said if she kept her colour she would be worth a mint. I shrugged, the filly was mine, and I was doubting she would **ever** be for sale. She was just special, I felt a bond like no other, the day I helped her mother birth her. Molly and I clicked, like two lost souls finding each other in the dark.

Then everything stopped, just as mysteriously as it started. The dreams, the tingling in my hands, the chats with the two-hundred-year-old. It all just vanished to be no more. I tried to call out to her a few times, but she never answered.

But she was right about the changing, by my fourteenth birthday, I was one hundred and eighty-five centimetres tall, I had ripped abs, a serious eight pack, not a six pack and arm and leg muscles most men spend hours at the gym trying to achieve.

It wasn't over done though... It was just a.... well, I am not sure how to describe it... but it certainly wasn't the muscles of a body builder. The strange part was I had done nothing really to get them. I put it down to all my hard work with the horses. My eyes had fully changed from mud brown to ice blue now, there was no hint of other colours anymore, and in certain lights they looked as if just the outside edge of the iris had blue, the rest was just ice colour. Framed by thick long black lashes. My hair was blacker then black, and thick and long to my shoulders. I had never had long hair before. Dad hated it and kept forcing me to cut it. He said I looked like a skeg (an old term for one who spent every waking minute surfing), and a bum, and that was unacceptable in his house. Trouble was if I had it cut, within a week, it had grown back. It never grew any longer than shoulder length though. I gave up trying to cut it, and I took to hiding it behind a hoodie, tucked under my shirt, so dad couldn't see it. My face shaped changed as well, no more rounded, it was now longer, leaner and I had a prominent chin, with a permanent five o'clock shadow. I was never short of a date, and girls followed me where ever I went.

It was about this time that dad told me I was going to be accompanying him to horse sales and shows. He could no longer manage on his own, and I needed to learn the family business that would one day be mine.

I loved the sales, the shows not so much. But that's how we got our name out, and how potential customers got to see what our horses could do.

More often than not the wives of our potential customers thought I was part of the deal, and several cornered me, and tried to bribe me into being intimate with them. I always refused, but some of them were pushy, and several times I only just managed to escape with my clothes and dignity intact.

My little filly Molly was coming along nicely and showing huge potential at just over a year old she was already seventeen hands high and was starting to get the defined muscles of her quarter horse mummy. Her colour not yet changed, was still chestnut with grey swirls. Her mane and tail were getting more purple strands in them all the time, they were almost one quarter purple now. One fine sunny day I wheeled Kevin out to see her. She wasn't a timid horse at all, she came right up to him and nuzzled her muzzle against his face and licked him. I could see his body moving with suppressed laughter, he had tears in his eyes, and he struggled and managed to give me a half thumbs up salute.
He had a smile on his face from ear to ear.

That night after I went to bed, I heard an unfamiliar male voice in my head. "Who's this?" I asked.

The voice replied with a laugh I am Kevin, silly.

What the hell.

I fell out of bed.

Chapter 5

"Kevin my brother?" I asked from the floor, wide awake now.

"Of course, who else do you know that is named Kevin?" he enquired.

"Wow, what, ummm how?" I asked confused. "The doctors said you have very limited brain activity, but you're talking to me in a normal voice, I have to say I'm a bit sceptical as to who you really are. Tell me something only you would know." I requested.

"When you were five and I was nine, and we were at the show in Brisbane, I stole two superhero show bags, one for you and one for me. And I told dad I found the money on the ground," he answered.

"Yup, I remember that, I was so scared we were going to get found out, but dad believed your story. How long have you been able to communicate like this and who else can hear you?" I asked.

"I have been trying for ages, there is important stuff I need to tell you and before we lose this connection. Joe, you need to know the nurse is an arse, he beats me all the time, he sticks me with needles when he shouldn't. He cuts my skin open. He pinches me, and sometimes he bites me. He swears and calls me all kind of names, including spastic. You have nearly caught him a few times, but in a blink of an eye he stops. Please Joe, don't leave me alone with him anymore."

"Kevin I am so sorry, I always suspected, but I could never prove anything, my poor poor brother I am so sorry. I will protect you when I can, but it's not enough. I have to go to school, and now to sales and shows with dad. I have a million chores plus every day. I don't know how I am going to protect you then." I was crying by the time I had finished speaking. I did not know what I was going to do. I had to tell dad that was for sure.

"He won't believe you, I rarely even see dad anymore, I know he blames himself for the way I am." Kevin replied.

"It's mum's fault he blames himself, because she still blames him," I replied nonchalantly.

"I know, I haven't lost my hearing, and I don't have limited brain activity, there is a severed connection between two areas of my brain, it can't be picked up on normal brain scans, because it hides close to the inner part of the skull. Under the brain. By being snapped it makes me unable to talk, it also causes the tic movements. My spinal cord is lacerated, and leaks spinal fluid into my back, that could be lasered closed, I still wouldn't be able to walk. I don't think. But if they fixed that and my brain, I would be able to use my hands, and talk, I would be a normal paraplegic. Instead of a total useless P O S."
"Don't say that," I snapped at him, "You're not a P O S, and don't believe anyone if they say you are. I continued a little quieter. "Now we need to come up with a plan, to get that moron out of your life. Kevin, **Kevin**, I called out in mind-speak."

Nothing, there was no answer. I got out of bed and raced to his room, he was sound asleep. No sign of movement or anything.

Well, that's about the weirdest thing ever I thought to myself.

I lay awake for hours that night, trying to think of a way to catch the nurse out. The fact he was and had been hurting my brother for years made me very angry, I was barely holding it together, I wanted to go find him and punch his head to a pulp.

I finally fell asleep in the early hours of the morning. I had nightmares most of the morning, and actually couldn't wait for my alarm to go off.

When it did and I got out of bed, I turned to pull my covers up, and noticed glitter in my bed.

Chapter 6

What the hell, I thought to myself, as if last night wasn't strange enough.

I wanted to check on Kevin as soon as I was able to this morning. So, I forgot the glitter and raced in to have a quick shower.

I went to my brothers' quarters, it was only 5 am, he hadn't been shifted out of bed into his chair yet. But he was awake. I pulled him up on his pillows so he was more sitting then lying, and offered him some of his water.

I asked him if he remembered talking to me last night. I was hoping he would answer in mind-speak, and that I could prove to myself I wasn't going crazy.

He stared at me blankly. I sighed, ok I was crazy. He started to make a fuss moving around as much as his body would allow and make a moaning/growling sound.
"Hey buddy," I tried to say as soothingly as possible, "Calm down, its ok."
I placed my hand on his shoulder, and he did, he calmed down. He looked down towards his hand that was lying by his side. I thought he wanted me to pick it up, but each time I tried he got agitated again. Then a light bulb went off in my mind, he had his thumb and he was trying to snag the hem of his shirt, he wanted me to lift his shirt. He looked at me and smiled. OK I thought, progress. I lifted the edge of his shirt up as high as I could. My knees buckled in shock, and for a moment I

thought I might fall down, at the shock of what I saw when I lifted his shirt. I couldn't believe what I was seeing, he had bruises, and small cuts and scratches, there was even a bite mark. I unbuttoned his shirt at the front and pulled it to the side, I was dumbfounded his whole chest and stomach was covered in sores, and cuts, some very deep, and looked like they should have been stitched. There were bite marks on his torso as well. I re-buttoned his shirt, I don't know why, but I did. I swore, I did not ever use that word, but it was the only one that was appropriate now. I cradled my brother in my arms, my tears falling on his hair.

"I'm so sorry," I said rocking him back and forth. Then suddenly I was angry, very angry. I let Kevin go, and gently laid him back on his bed. I told him it would be ok, that I would never let that bastard nurse hurt him again. I was ropeable, I think steam was coming out of my ears, and I knew my face had turned crimson. I was going to kill the nurse, the next time I saw that bastard he was going to die. I ran into dads' room, but he had already left. I banged on mum's door but the door was locked. What was I going to do? I raced outside hoping to catch dad in the stables. But his truck was already gone. While I was outside, I quickly did the minimum amount of my chores that I could. I fed and watered the horses under my care and I threw in some fresh bedding. I didn't have time to muck out the stalls today, and one day without it being done wouldn't hurt. I raced around and finished in record time. I ran back to my brother, grabbing a brekky milk carton from the fridge on the way past.

My plan was to stay with him today, and then talk to dad as soon as he got home. The nurse arrived at 8.30 am. He let himself into the house with the key he had been given. I was up, ready to kill him with my bare hands. Suddenly, the old fairy was in my head.

"Joe, please calm down, what you are about to do, won't help anybody." She said calmly to me via the mind talky thing.

"Bullshit," I snapped back.

"Joe, please!" She pleaded with me. "Just stop, breathe. I know you can do it, you are very strong, but think of the consequences, you have some amazing stuff in your future to look forward too. Do you really want to spend the rest of your life in jail? Who will be there for your brother then?"

"Where were you? You told me if I ever needed anything all I had to do was call you. I called you, you never came," I said accusingly.

I slumped against the wall, she was right, and I hated that more than anything. I wanted to be right. I wanted to feel ok with … Well if not actually killing, then at least seriously hurting the nurse. Like really hurting him, long hospital recovery kinda hurting, for all the years of torturing Kevin. And also, for my own guilt at not trusting my own gut feeling, when I knew something wasn't quite right with him. But no Andy was right, Kevin needed me, here, not locked up. I went back to Kevin's room and sat with him and waited for the nurse. Kevin had drifted back off to sleep. He looked so normal and peaceful in his sleep. I wanted to hold him forever and try and make him forgot the hell he had been through. The nurse got a shock when he walked into the room, and I was already there. "Bad night?" he asked me.

"You have no idea," I snarled at him, shifting my position so that I was sitting on my hands. I might have forgotten that I wasn't going to hurt him, if I didn't. I was still deciding, maybe I would wipe that smug look of his face after all.

"Careful," Andy said into my head, "Don't tip him off that you know what he has done. He might run, and then he will never pay for it."

I reluctantly, silently agreed with her.

I said to the nurse, "Yeah, I had some bad dreams, and just wanted to be with my bro today."

"He isn't your brother anymore, you know that right?" he said to me.

"Huh," I said, "Of course he is still my brother, and he always will be no matter what."

He replied matter-of-factly, with no emotion at all, "No he isn't, he is just a body with eyes, completely useless. He can't feel anything, can't communicate, he can't even feed himself he really just sucks in wasted air. He has no life at all. He just sits here all day waiting for someone like me to see to his every need. It would be so much easier if your family would just put him out of his misery."

I was getting very angry at what the nurse had just relayed to me.

"How dare you! That's my brother." I wanted to punch the guys head into the floor, how could anyone be so cold. "YOU KNOW NOTHING," I shouted at him.

Andy was speaking in my head saying, "Joe calm down, be careful what you say, we don't want to tip him off. He is just trying to make you get angry and leave the room, he can't hurt your brother while you're in here."

She was right as usual so I took a few deep breaths and forced myself to calm down. "I guess that's your opinion. Strange for you to be employed to look after patients like Kevin when that's what you think of them," I berated him.

"The job pays well and has its perks," he replied smirking.

It was taking all my self-control to not grab him by the neck and punch that smirk off his face. I could see tiny little specs falling in front of my face. It looked like really fine glitter dust. I put it down to dust flickering through the light coming into the room from the window. I thought the nurse was referring to how he was able to hurt my brother without anyone knowing, to feed his sadistic side. But I was soon to find out he was meaning a whole lot more than just my brother.

Mum stuck her head around Kevin's doorway about 10.30 am, asked the nurse how he (Kevin) was today, she said morning to me, then said she would be in the stables today, working with her mare. She had a huge smile on her face. I don't think I had seen her smile for a long, long time. She left before I had even had a chance to tell her I needed to talk to her. I thought about running after her, but I did not want to leave Kevin alone with the nurse any longer then was absolutely necessary.

I sat with Kevin all morning, much to the nurses' disgust. I helped get him out of bed, then nurse shooed me out of the room when he was changing him. I protested, but he said he needed the room around Kevin to manoeuvre him, and had to be able to grab him quickly if he was going to fall. I moved to the doorway, and the nurse made sure he kept himself in the way, so I couldn't see Kevin's naked body at any time. I watched him have his treatments, and be spoon fed his food. Kevin had a modified tablet, it was rather large, and extra thick, with a soft bouncy cover on it, so as if it got knocked to the floor it wouldn't break. The tablet was full of activities for Kevin to do, simple counting and maths, word associations etc. or he could just watch a movie on it. Just after Kevin had eaten his lunch and the nurse set him up with his tablet, he told me he was going out for his break. I waited until he had left, then I left Kevin as well, I told him via mind-speak, I wasn't sure if he could still hear me or not, but it was worth a try, that I was going to find mum.

Chapter 7

I raced out to the stables for the second time today. When I entered the stables all the horses called out greetings to me as they always did and they stuck their noses over the doors of their pens and expected pats. I had no time today though, I did not know how long the nurse would be away for, and I didn't want him spending any more time alone with my brother. I could hear strange noises coming from the tack room, I opened the door, and there was mum, with the nurse. Catching dad kissing the last nurse was one thing, what mum was doing with this nurse, was a whole other ball game. I don't know who had more of a shock. But I was mortified. That's something a child should never see not even when it is his own parents. I slammed the door and ran outside. I took a few minutes to calm myself down, then I made my way back to my brother. I was just about inside, when I heard the stable door bang and mum running out calling after me. I stopped and waited for her. "Don't bother," I said to her and held my hand up to her face. "I don't want to hear it. You stopped being my mother when you had the accident, always too caught up in yourself. You couldn't even see how much you kept tearing dad apart by always blaming him for the accident, but you know what mum, unlike what I just caught you doing. The car crash, it really was an accident. AND IT WAS NO ONE'S FAULT! You destroyed our family long before now, this is just the top of the cake."

I started to walk away, "Oh and by the way, dad **will** be hearing about this." I said looking back over my shoulder.

 I went back and sat with Kevin. The nurse returned to finish his shift, I didn't think he would have the guts to, but he did. It was awkward, I didn't look at him, and I didn't speak to him.

It was 5:10pm when I heard dad's big ute pull up, the nurse had just left and Kevin was resting. I ran out to meet dad, the ute was full up of bags of horse food. I started to help him unload the bags. I had a little chuckle to myself, the bags were 40kgs each and I could throw them around like foot balls. As we were unloading, I said to dad, "I have some stuff to tell you. It's very important but you need to see it, while I explain it."

"Sounds serious, is it the reason you didn't go to school today?" he asked sternly.

"Yeah kinda," I replied, shrugging.

The ute was unloaded in record time.

"Ok let's go see what kept grade ten's star pupil out of the class room today." Dad commented.

We washed our hands and headed inside, I led him to Kevin's room, he stalled a bit.

"DAD, he's your son. I know it hurts you to see him the way he is, but it hurts him more by you not spending time with him," I shrugged.

Knowing I was over stepping the boundary. One did not tell my father how to live his life, or contradict any of his decisions.

I was waiting for the tongue lashing, and possible clip behind the ear, that I would normally receive for voicing my opinion. It didn't come, dad just shrugged and opened Kevin's door.

When we walked in Kevin was still resting, dad turned to leave and I shook my head and pulled him back. I tapped Kevin on the shoulder, "Hey buddy," I said gently. He opened his eyes and smiled, his version of a smile when he saw us. I said to him, "I'm just going to show dad what we discussed this morning ok buddy."

He blinked twice which was his signal for ok or yes. I pulled his t-shirt up to his chin and stepped out of the way so dad could see.

"**What the holy hell!**" dad yelled out, with a mixture of shock and alarm. "**Where did all that came from? Who the f&&^%% has been torturing my son. My poor boy**." Dad went over to Kevin and hugged him, dad was crying, and rocking Kevin, "My son, my poor boy."

Dad turned to me and asked me how I knew? I explained to him that he wouldn't believe me, but told him I seen it in a dream. I also told him that part of the dream was about a severed connection between two areas of his brain, and how it couldn't be picked up on normal brain scans. It hides close to the inner part of the skull, under his brain, if surgeons could find a way to re attach it, he would have full brain activity again. His spinal cord is lacerated, and leaks spinal fluid into his back. The leak could be lasered closed.

He just nodded. I don't think he was really even listening to me. He was in shock over seeing his son in the state he was in. Dad moved away, he called out, "WENDY! Get your arse in here now."

I was having a private laugh to myself. I know the timing was wrong, and I shouldn't be amused, but I knew she was going to think I had told dad what I had seen today in the stables. She entered the room, her head down and her shoulders slumped. She was waiting for dad to yell at her for having an affair.

I left. Not far though, just to the kitchen. It was far enough that I couldn't really hear dad talking, just murmurs of sound. I did hear mum exclaim, and then burst into tears. "What do we do?" she asked dad. I'm not sure if she was really upset at what had been happening to Kevin, or just relived that it wasn't about her extra marital events.

Dad went by me to the phone, and called the police, then Kevin's physician. When dad left the room, I threatened her, I told her if she breathed a word of this to lover boy, before we had a chance to catch him and make him pay for what he had done to Kevin, I would make her life hell forever more.

Through her tears she said, "I honestly did not know he was hurting Kevin, Joe. I know you think I am a monster, but there is no way am I ever going to see that nurse again. It doesn't matter what you think of me I am still your mother. Believe it or not I do and always have had you and your brothers' best interest at heart. Please Joe, let's forget about what you saw this morning. I promise you it will never happen again!"

I shrugged at her, and looked her straight in the eye and remarked, "I doubt you have cared about any member of this house hold, except yourself, since the accident, and that wouldn't have changed in the last five minutes."

She spluttered a bit and eventually pleaded "Joe please, don't ruin our family any more than it already has been. You're a growing man now, but there are somethings you still wouldn't understand, this is one of them. I could try to explain to you, but I know your hurting right now, and I doubt you would be able to see my side of the equation. But believe me when I tell you there are always two sides to a story. Please Joe, your father has enough to deal with now, don't add an extra burden on him!"

I looked at her silently, and just walked away to my brother's room.

The doctor got here a few minutes before the police. Photos were taken, documents were filled out. Evidence was collected. I tried to get the doctor to listen to me about how to fix Kevin, he replied he had never heard of any such area of the brain, and that they couldn't fix spinal cord leakages with laser therapy, it had been tried. I begged him to just try, I knew dad would pay for the operation, and surely it was worth a try. The doctor said he would look into it. We gave the police the file we had on the nurse, with his full name, address, next of kin etc., and then they left to find him and were going to officially charge him. We received a phone call a couple hours later, saying everything he told us was a lie, there was no such person by that name, and the address and next of kin details were all fake. Dad started to get agitated, thinking we would never catch him.

"Dad he will turn up here for work in the morning, he is an arrogant son of a bitch. He would never imagine for one second that he had been caught out. We'll get the bastard then," I assured him.

Dad phoned the police back and told them I thought he might still turn up for work in the morning. They agreed that if he did turn up in the morning, they would arrest him then. They were going to have a police car here early, waiting at the back of our property. I never let mum know this as I no longer trusted her.

Sure enough at 8.30 am on the dot, the motor bike came down the driveway. A police officer entered the house via a back door and stood out of site.

The nurse let himself in. He didn't see us in the kitchen, he went straight to Kevin's room, but never made it, the police had him on the floor and in hand cuffs within seconds. They then took him away in a police car. Mum came into the kitchen, and poured herself a coffee, she had missed all the action. Dad told her matter-of-factly that the nurse was now gone, and they would have to sort Kevin out until a replacement could be found.

I chose then to tell dad about mum and the nurse. I was fifteen, almost sixteen, my reasoning chip hadn't fully engaged in my brain, and to tell the truth, I never wanted to see her again. I blamed her, if she had of spent more time with Kevin instead of fluttering here there and everywhere, and having relations with the hired help, she would have seen what was happening long ago.

"Dad," I said, "Yesterday morning when I found out all this was going on."

Mum was staring at me her eyes pleading with me, to not say anything.

"I ran to your room to tell you, but you had already left. I then went to mum's door and knocked, but the door was locked and she either did not hear or ignored me. So, I had to wait until the nurse had his lunch break. Then I found mum and the nurse naked in each other's arms in the tack room."

Dad stared at me, "You are kidding right?"

"Nope," I shrugged. I looked my mother straight in the eyes the whole time I was telling dad of her exploits.

He turned to mum, "Wendy is that true?"

Mum had tears running down her face, and all she could do was nod.

"I want you out of my house, by 5 pm tonight, don't even think about trying to take the house or business, or try and get money out of me. The moment we moved to separate rooms, every single asset we had, was signed into Joe's name. And you won't get a cent, all you will get is anything here that you own, that you brought with your own money, oh wait that's right, you never had your own money. Not even when you were teaching dance, every cent you earnt plus more went into the up keep of your studio. And don't try and say you helped run the stud, because you haven't worked a day with any horse here, except your own mare. THAT I GIFTED TO YOU, to try and get you interested in the business. I will allow you to keep your brand new 4x4, nothing else," he told her flatly.

"So, you knew?" I said to dad.

"I suspected she was being unfaithful with someone, I just didn't know who, and couldn't prove anything, and I never would have dreamed it was a nurse employed to take care of our son," dad said bitterly.

"I guess you did it too, just not to the same extent, with a nurse hired to look after him," I said.

'NO, I DID NOT," dad shouted at me, "It was all a lie, that kiss your mother saw, was the first and only one, AND FOR THE RECORD SHE KISSED ME."

"Ok, not sure why you had to yell at me though, I didn't do it!" I said and stormed off.

I could hear him apologising as I walked away.

Mum left in her almost brand new 4x4 in the early hours of the next morning. After her and dad had been up all-night yelling at each other, each blaming the other one for the total breakdown of their marriage. In the end mum was begging and pleading with dad to change his mind, and give her another chance, she promised she would change, she swore to him she would never stray again, she said she would become the perfect wife. Just as she was leaving,

I heard her threaten dad, she said, "He would regret throwing her onto the street, with no money and nowhere to stay other than the back of her car."

He angrily pointed out, "You should think you're lucky to even have that!"

I went to bed but I never slept, their argument was loud, and I doubt anyone with in a ten-kilometre radius hadn't heard it. After mum stormed off up the driveway, I heard dad slam the house door, and go into his stables.

I laid awake wondering how we would ever get anything done, now that the nurse was gone and it was just dad and I, how were we going to look after Kevin **and** the horse stud? I still had to go to school. Dad couldn't do it all on his own. He might have to hire a couple of people to help with the stable chores, but I wouldn't let them near Molly, they would need to understand she was off limits, to everyone but me.

Chapter 8

The next morning I slept in, it was well after 9am when I jumped up with a fright, damn I had missed school again. Twice in one week. Dad wouldn't be impressed. At least I would be home today to help with all the extra chores, I thought to myself. I stumbled out to the kitchen, to my surprise Grandma and Aunty Denny were having coffee and croissants. I joined them and I hugged my Grandma and my Aunty. I hadn't seen my grandma for over three years, she left just before I turned twelve. I hadn't seen my Aunty in double that number of years. Grandma couldn't believe I was the same skinny boy she had last seen. She kept looking at me and saying things like, "What have you been eating boy? And are you sure you are my little Joe, the boy who used to sit on my knee and let me read to him every night?"

"Yes Grandma," I laughed embarrassed at all the attention.

Dad had phoned both Grandma and Aunty Denny last night, after mum had left and they had decided that Aunty Denny was going to stay and help with Kevin and dad was also going to be spending more time with Kevin, and helping Aunty Denny out.

Between all of us, there would be no more need for nurses. Dad told me I was going to have to do more around the place. I would need to feed, water and muck out the stalls for all the horses, at the moment this included his as well. He also informed me, he was going to hire some builders to build a second set of stables and a second arena, with a 'show room' off of it. The new stables would be in the paddock to the right side of the house, the show room would be within close walking distance of that end of the house, where dads study was. He wanted a room where we could showcase all the achievements our horses had gained, ribbons, trophies, best in show awards, and race placings, etc., to show prospective buyers, our horses potentials, and his study was getting too small. The new stables would be mine, and would have a dozen stalls, to house my horses, including ones I would breed from my new mare in the coming years.

My new chores list also included working any horses that dad did not get a chance to work, when I got home from school. He wanted mum's mare sold, as soon as I was able too. She apparently told him she never wanted her. I begged him to let her stay, this was her home. Reluctantly he agreed. I was given a very stern warning, that my school grades had better not start to suffer from the extra work I had to do and if there was even the slightest drop, he would take Molly away from me. Might as well kill me then, I thought to myself, that horse was the only thing that kept me going. I told dad that maybe we had been looking at the whole situation wrong, and that maybe instead of hiring a nurse for Kevin we should have hired help for the stud, that way no one would be so tired out.

Dad informed me that he had made a decision last night, that no matter how hard things got, **we**

were never hiring any more help. It just led to trouble we didn't need.

Aunt Denny sighed and winked at me, "Pity, I could do with some cowboy eye candy to look at around here," she said teasingly.

Dad sent her a scathing look, "If you really want eye candy sister, perhaps you can start coming to the horse shows, and helping out," he said seriously.

She screwed her face up at his back as he walked away.

Grandma was going to move back into her old cottage, and no matter how much we protested, she wouldn't have it any other way. But we did come to a compromise that in bad weather, she would stay here at the house.

Dad told me today was the last day I would have off school for the rest of the year, and that he had already done my chores for me this morning. He also told me sometime today he wanted to speak to me about Molly.

"Yes sir, thank-you," I replied.

I went back to my room, to tidy it up, and make my bed. I thought I might do some catch up maths. I also had a pile of washing on the floor, to take to the laundry. As I was gathering the dirty laundry and tiding up my room, I noticed glitter everywhere. It was in my bed, on my floor, over my shelves and all through the pile of washing on the floor and in my bathroom. What the hell? Where has all that come from? I hated glitter! Sparkly things drew attention to one's self, and I hated attention, and I got more than enough attention with my looks anyway, and glitter was for girls. The glitter was a mystery, I searched high and low for the source of it but came up empty handed.

I finished cleaning my room, dusted and vacuumed, got rid of as much of the glitter as I could find, and took my washing to the laundry. Grandma saw the washing pile and asked me what I was planning on doing with it? I sheepishly told her I had been really busy with other stuff and this was a few weeks' worth and I hadn't learnt to use the washing machine yet.

She butted in and said, "Well my boy, if you really are my boy, and not some Alien that's taken over him, there is no time like the present to learn."

She followed me to the laundry, showed me how to separate the clothes, how much detergent and softener to put in, and how to set the machine, and how to make the machine start. As we were sorting through the first load, glitter was falling everywhere I was very embarrassed, grandma laughed at all the glitter and said to me, "Has the glitter fairy been visiting you boy?" "It's highly possible, coz I have no other explanation for all of it," I said, my cheeks burning red hot.

Grandma walked out giggling to herself, about boys trying to be men before they were ready to be.

I spent the day working my horses. Molly was the most beautiful mare I had ever seen, her colours still vivid and unchanged, she was super friendly, and smart. I couldn't wait until she was saddle broken. I had plans of showing her.

 As soon as I was able to, I was going to put my dapple grey, over Molly's mum's sister, I was curious to see if the colour varied. Molly's mum's sister was not quite the chocolate brown, she was more a muddy chestnut.

At lunch time, I went to dad's office and knocked on the door, he beckoned me to go in. I sat on the spare chair and waited for him to finish on the phone. When he did, he told me he had been speaking to the police and they had told him that the nurse had been formally charged. He was to be held in prison at least until his hearing in a few months' time. Dad added, that no bail had been set, because he was a flight risk.

"That's good news, I hope the bastard gets life, it's just unfortunate we don't have the death penalty in Australia," I added.

Dad nodded in agreement, "Sometimes in this world son, there just isn't the right amount of justice."

Dad wanted to know all about Molly and her training so far, her statistics, height, weight, any signs of weaknesses, or things that could be potential problems in the future. How much weight she was gaining weekly. How she was taking to the lunging rein, her foot fall count, everything.

I told him as much as I could and he wrote it all down in a journal. She is not for sale he told me, not ever, she is going to be breeding stock. She has everything we need to move the quarter horses forward, to a new era.

I told him I wasn't planning on selling her. She was special, everything about her was special. I also made it very clear to him, that she was my horse, not his.

Later that night I went into Kevin's room, I told him what happened to the nurse, he looked happy. We will just have to wait and see what the judge does in four months' time. I read more of the wizard story to him, until he fell asleep. I fell asleep in the chair in his room.

When my Aunty woke me the next morning, the sun was shining through the curtains. "Didn't your dad tell you no more days off school young man?" "Shit, yeah," I said and jumped up.

She laughed at me, and cautioned me on the use of my language.

 "A man should never have to prove how much of a man he is by having to resort to foul language. All it does is bring him down to a level he should never stoop too," She informed me.

I looked at my watch, damn it was only 6am.

I looked up at her and she winked at me, "You have chores right. Joe," she called out as I was leaving, "What the hell is all this sparkly mess all over the damn place, are you turning into a unicorn and farting glitter now?"

I didn't even reply, I just left the room mortified.

The next week-end I entered molly in a horse show, she took out every prize and won best in show. I had people coming up to me the whole time they were there asking to buy her. Some offered me hundreds of thousands of dollars for her. I ended up having to put a sign up on her stall, stating she wasn't for sale. I told dad that afternoon when he came to pick her up. He asked if I had got the name and phone numbers of those who offered the most money for her, of course I said to him. Almost every week-end from then on, I took her to shows. She loved the attention, and whenever she got a new ribbon or rosette, she pranced around showing it off.

Occasionally we would make it a family outing and Grandma, Aunty and Kevin would come too. It was very tiring for him, but you could see he loved being there, and would even try to eat a Dagwood dog. Molly had a special bond with Kevin, she was always happy to see him, and she would break her tie rope to get to him, and nuzzle his face with hers.
She would lick his face like a big dog would do.

Often, she would kneel herself down and place her head in his lap, so as he could pat her. Have I mentioned how much of a gentle sole my horse was? I know Kevin would have given anything to be able to ride her.

I suggested to dad that we should get Kevin a dog. Dad vetoed the idea saying we had enough animals to look after as it was.

A few months later we had our day in court, the judge sentenced the nurse to the term of his natural life, {or twenty-five years} which ever came first, never to be paroled, he said his crime was heinous and shameful and the nurse showed no remorse.

I talked to Molly a lot and one day I asked her about Kevin having a ride on her, she nuzzled my chest and whinnied softly, then she knelt down with front and back legs folded, so as her back was less than a half a metre off the ground. She seemed really satisfied with herself. I nodded, I was strong enough to lift him that distance.

I had to wait until dad and Aunty were busy, if they saw what I was doing, or got an inkling of what I was planning they would go ballistic.

It took almost a week to have Kevin to myself for a few hours, it was a Saturday, dad was off seeing a potential buyer. I faked a cold, so he didn't take me with him. Aunty Denny and Grandma were off doing the grocery shopping. I wheeled Kevin out to Molly's stable, and in through the gate. Luckily the ground was compacted and it was easy enough to push his chair through. When Molly saw Kevin she came running over from the other side of her paddock, and skidded to a halt just centimetres from where we were, throwing dust everywhere. Kevin smiled at her, and tried to reach out to pat her. Molly turned side on to us and did her kneel down thing, I picked Kevin up out of his chair. I knew he couldn't sit straight up on her, so I laid him tummy side down across her back, with his head out one side and his feet dangling out the other side. I climbed up behind him and locked him in place with my legs. "Ok," I said to Molly.

Very, very slowly one leg at a time she stood up. When she was upright, she moved off in the most awkward walk you have ever seen, it was like she was almost trying to tip toe, she was trying very hard not to jostle around too much, so as Kevin wouldn't fall. "It's ok," I whispered to her, "I got him, he won't fall."

She started to walk normally and we walked around for about an hour. several times I dismounted to make sure Kevin was ok. The first time I checked on him, he had the biggest smile on his face that I had ever seen, and tears streaming down his face. "I hope they are happy tears," I told him. He blinked twice.

When it was time for him to go back in his chair, Molly repeated the whole kneeling process, very slowly one leg at a time. Kevin never even moved at all she did such a good job of it. I carried him back to his chair and let him watch while I brushed her down and praised her.

Chapter 9

My seventeenth birthday came and went, without a big fuss. I took my girlfriend on a date to the movies, and asked her to the horse show the next day. Dad brought me a brand new 4x4 ute, and a new horse float with the studs' banner on the sides and Molly's pictured, painted on the banner. She was our new logo. I didn't have my license yet, but would soon, and dad said it was time I learnt how to drive safely with a float hooked to the car. I did not argue, after everything I guess it was only normal he wanted me to get lots of practise at that.

I had taken Kevin for quite a few rides, and I'm sure he looked forward to them as much as I did. We always rode bareback, I really think Kevin loved the feel of Molly under him, and not a hard saddle. Now I sat him up straight, I got on behind him, I used my body and arms to support his back, wrapping my arms under his to hold onto the reins. I still locked my legs around his, with him sitting up it was easy to keep his legs firmly against Molly's side with my legs. Molly was voice trained as well as squeeze trained, which meant I didn't really need to use reins, a slight push of my leg against one of her sides and she knew to turn that way. I could tell her what I wanted, walk on, trot, or canter up and she would do it. When we finished the ride, I stayed with him on Molly's back until she had done her kneeling thing, then I would slide Kevin off before me, and prop him up on her side, before dismounting and carrying him to his chair. It took a few times to get his balance on Molly's side just right, the first couple of times, by the time I had dismounted, he had fallen down and had been laying on his side, in a sitting position, on the grass, with Molly trying to grab at him with her mouth to pull him back up again.

I was still fighting a losing battle with the glitter, it would end up all through Molly's mane and tail, every time I got her ready for a show.

I was able to saddle her and ride her now. She was super-fast and very sure on her feet, so as well as showing we did things like calf roping and barrel racing now. She never lost. And still did the little prance whenever she won a ribbon, which was always. Dad insisted all her trophies, ribbons, newspaper articles etc., went to the room he had had built for that purpose. He showed the room off to anyone who ever came to our place. Especially those looking to acquire our horses.

In the last couple of years, I have had a couple of spills and had broken a few bones. Once I got trampled by a cow. At these times I always had the fairy Andy in my head, helping ease my pain. After I was trampled by the cow, I swear she was in the hospital room with me. I'm not sure how I escaped without serious injuries, or scaring.

Kevin was just days away from his twenty-first birthday, and I had something special planned for him. By some miracle Molly had come into season at exactly the right time that if she got pregnant then, the foal would be born on or a couple days either side of Kevin's birthday. I was going to give the foal to him. I was excited to see Molly's first foal. I had bred her by artificial insemination. I had been to the Arabian horse stud that my dappled grey had come from, and I had paid a fortune for the seed of an unrelated huge dark grey Arab stallion.

The night before Kevin's twenty-first birthday, for the first time in years, he mind spoke to me. ESP'd he called it. He thanked me for dealing with the nurse, said he was finally able to rest easy at night now, knowing that bastard would never hurt anyone again. He told me how much he loved riding Molly, and how much it helped him mentally, to be able to be on a horse again. He told me he loved me, and that he was so glad I was his little brother. He said he was very proud of the man I was becoming. He said he wished me only good things in my life. He also told me one day a woman was going to come along and knock my socks off, she would be the love of my life and she would fix everything about myself that I didn't like. He remarked I was a really good guy, and always would be, and to never let anyone bring me down. And Joe, never be afraid to ask for help, this stubborn arsed attitude of never asking for help has to stop. He said there was going to come a time when I would need help, and if I didn't ask for it, lives would be lost. He also explained, I would meet another girl, who would drive me to distraction, and would call me cowboy, and I would love her more than my own life, but not as much as the woman I was with. I would almost cross a line with her, but at the last minute I would come to my senses, I would take it upon myself to be the knight in shining armour for both of these females and I would lay down my own life for theirs if called upon to do so. He explained that there would be a couple of very important male figures come into my life, and I would have an instant connection with them, feeling as though I had known them for my whole life. I would form an unbreakable bond with them within minutes of meeting them. One of them was going to need my help in a big way. They were both going to be attracted to my special girl, but I would not feel any jealousy towards them. Kevin told me it would be ok for me to call them brothers, and that it would honour him, as both of these males would have exceptional characteristics, and have the same morals and standards that he does. They would also lay down their lives for myself and the two women, as I would for all of them.

He told me that for what was to come, to not fret or be to upset as I had made his life bearable for the last twelve years. He started to laugh then and said he remembered the first time I had snuck into his room after the accident, with his magic wand tucked under my arm, a stream of multi-coloured ribbons falling out of the wand, trailing behind me as I walked into his room. He said it was the best thing anyone had even done for him, and no matter where he was, he would never forget it.

I did not understand anything he was saying or why he was saying it. I had a girlfriend, I liked her, but I knew deep down she wasn't the one. I would never cheat on any girl, I had seen how that scenario played out, with our mother and father, and no way would I do that to anyone. Kevin interrupted my thoughts and said, "You won't cheat. The girl who completes you will not be jealous of the other, and will love her the same as you do."

I thought maybe it was a daughter.

"No!" Kevin interrupted again. "You will have a daughter but that's going to be a long way off, and she will be loved and protected by many."

I was more confused than ever now and then my mind went silent.

"Kevin," I called, but there was no reply.

You know sometimes in life when you wish you had of held on a little longer, stalled for more time, asked more questions. This was one of those times.

Chapter 10

The next morning Kevin had moved to the eternal sleep, on the day he would have celebrated his twenty-first birthday, he was gone, to live forever more in the afterlife. Sometime through the night he had suffered a massive stroke.

The conversation I had shared with him last night came flooding back to me, he knew, he knew he was dying. I never said goodbye, I never told him I loved him, I never told him how proud I was of how hard he fought. For a fleeting second, I heard his voice in my head, "I know bro, I know."

"NO WAIT, PLEASE DON'T LEAVE ME," I screamed out in mind-speak. But he was gone.

It didn't sink in, I couldn't believe he was gone, I guess we always knew, after the accident the doctors gave him five years and he had more than that, I guess we should be thankful, but I couldn't believe he was gone. The house started filling up, there were doctors and ambos and people everywhere. Sometime around mid-morning, mum turned up. She looked a mess. No more salon nails or hair. The clothes were from a large variety store not a designer dress shop.

I retreated to the stables, I couldn't be around all those people right now, especially not my mother. When I got to the stables, I could see Molly was in the early stages of labour. I made myself useful helping her, rubbing her swollen belly, making her walk around the stables, and talking to her gently, telling her how she was the best horse in the world, trying to soothe her. My little foal that was to be a gift to my big brother, was going to make its entrance into the world sometime today.

The little colt was born at 5:50pm. Molly did not have an easy time of it, half way through I had to ring the vet, and get her to race out to our place. The foal had somehow got stuck inside, and no matter how much I maneuvered Molly's' belly, I couldn't dislodge the foal. I thought I was going to lose the foal and Molly. It was touch and go for a while and the vet told me to prepare for the worst. But surely the universe couldn't be that mean. She pulled through but needed to go onto antibiotics for a couple of weeks. The little colt when he finally made his entrance into the world, was very weak, and I had to hold him so as he could have his first feed. He was the complete opposite colour of his mother, instead of being brown with grey swirls, he was grey with chocolate swirls, and his mane and tail was definitely a shade of lilac. He was spectacular. I sat on the floor of her stall and patted my little mare, "Good job," I told her my voice soothing her. I looked down at her unique colouring, she had glitter all over her. "How the hell?" I asked her.

Andy's voice jumped into my mind and she said she was sorry about my brother, but he was in a better place now.

She told me that although I didn't know it yet, it was the glitter saved molly.

"Sure it was," I answered sarcastically.

"Soon now, I promise Joe, stay strong, it won't be long," then she was gone.

I was totally exhausted, and still had adrenaline pumping through my system. I went inside and headed straight for Kevin's room. I had been in the stables for hours, I wanted to tell him about the foal. I actually got as far as the kitchen, when I remembered, he was gone. It was then, that exact moment, that the reality hit me. I stood there, in the kitchen hall way and tears just streamed uncontrollably down my face and I couldn't breathe. I felt my heart break in two. Someone wrapped their arms around me and stood there just holding me. I couldn't stop crying or sobbing. He was gone, he was really gone. I sunk to the floor, my legs unable to hold me up any longer.

"It's ok son," dad said, "We were blessed to have an extra twelve years with him."

I wasn't going to answer that, for most of those twelve years he lived in pain, and he was being tortured by a sadistic bastard.

Just then Andy's voice was in my head, "There was good times for him too Joe, and good memories for you too. Memories you will carry with you for life."

"I can't do it," I said to Andy. "How do I manage without him? I miss him already."

"One day at a time, you will never forget but it will get easier," she answered.

I walked out of the house, and headed to the stables because I couldn't face the...... house. I just couldn't be in there anymore.

Molly's little colt was tentatively standing, he was very wobbly. As I sat on the floor of molly's stall, the little guy fell over a couple of times. I couldn't help myself but I laughed at his awkwardness. Molly nudged me, as if she was telling me not to laugh at him. I agreed with her, and stroked her muzzle. The little colt was as curious as his mother and within an hour he was standing over my head, smelling my hair. He needed a name. My brothers middle name was Harry, and it was the perfect name for the foal. Molly agreed, as soon as I thought of the name, she licked me. Yup, ok, Harry it is then.

Grandma entered the stables a couple hours later and she called out to me. I stood up and told her where I was. She brought me over a sandwich and a coffee. I was grateful for the coffee but not sure if I could eat though. Andy mind-speaking, "You need to keep your strength. EAT the sandwich." I ate the sandwich.

I showed my new foal to grandma. She couldn't find the words to describe him, but she gushed and gooed over him. I told her his name was Harry. She hugged me and said with tears in her eyes, "It was fitting." She took my empty dishes and then left me alone.

I left the stall and went to do my other chores. I wasn't sure if dad had done his work today, so I checked his stock, and made sure they had food and water. One day without exercise wouldn't hurt them.

By the time I finished the chores it was late, and there was no moon in the sky, so all the paddocks were black, the only lights were coming from the house or my stables. I turned the lights out in dad's stables when I finished bedding down his horses. I didn't go to the house. I still couldn't face the sadness there. I wasn't up to dealing with people yet either, everyone meant well I know, but I just wasn't sure I could deal with the small talk right now. I went straight to my stables, to check on Molly. I noticed there was still a bunch of cars in the driveway. Most I didn't recognise, but I did notice mum's was still there.

When I walked into Molly's stall, Harry was having his dinner and Molly quietly neighed at me. She was so proud. I sat in the corner of her stall. "Sorry girl," I said to her, "I just don't want to be in the house right now."

I looked at the ground at the piles of glitter. Harry had glitter all over him. I shook my head, and looked at molly, "I don't know," I said sighing, answering her silent question. I could hear a horse whinnying, it was coming from the paddock behind my stables. I got up to check it out. My stallion was stamping the ground and snorting, and calling out. I climbed through the fence into his pen.

"What's wrong buddy?" I said, as I walked up to him as he was super agitated. I started to pat his neck and tried to calm him down, but he wasn't having any of it. He was stamping his feet and jumping around, twice he nearly landed on me. He was throwing his head around as well. I left him and walked around his pen because I thought there may been a snake in his pen, or a dingo nearby. He followed me round his pen walking behind me, nuzzling my back everytime I stopped to look at something. I found nothing. I walked back to where I had climbed through the fence. I patted the stallion again and this time he calmed a bit. I went back to the stable. I slept in the stall with Molly and Harry. I awoke sometime during the night with Harry lying curled up against my back and Molly's head on my chest. I was freezing cold but I wasn't going to move and disturb them. I put one arm behind my head and drifted back off to sleep. Sometime through the night someone threw a thick wool blanket over me and the horses.

Chapter 11

The glitter was getting out of control. I had just turned eighteen. The glitter was driving me nuts, every day I was cleaning it from the floor, the bed, the lounge, the stables.

"Honestly enough already!" I screamed in my mind to Andy. Andy and I had become best friends in the last few months, although we had never actually met. I had seen her numerous times in my dreams though. She was pretty, dressed in the same off white long old-fashioned dress, and she had apple green wings. Classic fairy shaped wings just like cartoon fairies have.

Sometimes I dreamt of others like her as well, ones older than me, and other times they are younger than me. All the people are fairies, and they all have wings. There is one with blue hair that I dream about a lot.

Grandma has moved back into the house now and has taken Kevin's rooms. She had a fall in the cottage six months ago when the creek was in flood, and no one knew about it for a week. Dad put his foot down and said either she moved into the main house or he would put her in a home. Kevin's room had been cleaned out two months after his death and everything was either thrown out or given to charity. I kept his magic cards, and his magic kits. Not much for twenty-one years, but I know they meant the world to him. I had thrown myself into work to help distract me from the still raw emotion I felt at losing my brother. I was showing Molly and now Harry under lead, every week-end.

I have had my license for almost a year, and I was driving myself to the shows, no longer relying on my father. My aunt was still living here, she said we needed looking after. She was our cook, house cleaner etc. and she made sure grandma got to any appointments she had. Dad retreated into his study and I rarely saw him anymore, unless something was wrong, I understand now how Kevin felt.
Exactly twelve months to the day Kevin died, I had a visit from Andy, an actual in the flesh, her standing in my room visit.

"Up Joe!" she told me, you're about to get a crash course in what your glitter is all about. I stumbled out of bed, with only my pyjama bottoms on. Andy took a sharp breath in, "Hmmm," she remarked, "The male glitter fairy body is never disappointing. It's just a shame I am your mentor, because I would give anything to run my hands over those abs."

"Nothing stopping you," I told her with a cheeky wink.

The two-hundred and something-year-old fairy actually blushed.

"Come on you, I always imagined you were going to be trouble with a capital T," she replied laughing.

It was rhetorical, she wasn't expecting a reply. I flashed her my 100 watt smile instead. She blew some glitter in my face and too my surprise my pyjamas got replaced with my jeans and a too tight t-shirt. I laughed cheekily pulling at the t-shirt.

"Concentrate," she said. "Shrug your shoulders a few times. Hmmm, try rolling your shoulders. Ok, they are being a bit stubborn." I raised my eye brows at her.

"Stand still," she commanded.

She walked around behind me, "Uh huh," she said.

"You're checking out my butt aren't you?" I asked her.

"Sure am," she replied unashamedly.

She flicked my shoulder blades.

"Ouch," I flinched.

"Wait for it, just wait," she replied.

"Oh, ow OUCH omg holy mother of," I started to say. As a pain like I had never known ripped across my shoulders to half way down my back.

Andy blew some glitter across my shoulders and the pain eased a little, until I could bear it.

"Shake your shoulders again," miss bossy commanded.

I did, and a pair of black wings unfolded from my back. They were made from what looked like unbreakable spiders' silk, they also looked like a spider's web delicate and intricate. They glimmered in the light every time I moved them.

I turned to Andy, "Are these really mine?"

She mysteriously replied, "Let's hope so."

"YEAH!!" I cheered and punched the air.

"Do they work? Can I fly?" I enquired sceptically.

"Give them a try," Andy responded.

I stared at her, "Um how?"

"Flap them, concentrate on bringing them in and out," she explained, blowing glitter on my new wings.

"Ooooookay," I tried what she said. I was lifting of the ground, higher and higher until my head banged into the ceiling.

She pulled my leg and pulled me back to the ground.

"Piece of cake," I grinned at her.

"Huh huh," she said, rolling her eyes grinning.

She sighed and led me through a doorway that did not exist in my wall three hours ago. When we were outside, she said, "Now follow me."

She flew into the air and I followed her. I was a bit awkward for a few minutes, but then it was as natural as riding a horse.

I heard Andy mumble, "Of course" in her mind.

I chuckled.

We flew to an older part of Surfers Paradise, to an old weather board house.

Andy said, "Remember the dreams Joe, the ones with the little kids?"

"Yeah, so there is a little kid here being bullied?" I asked.

"Yes, the little girl is wheel chair bound, she was born with problems with the bones in her legs. And can't stand or walk on her own, she can stand if she has something to hold on to. She's bright and bubbly, and the friendliest little girl you will ever meet. She attends a special gymnastics class, where she gets to learn stretches, ribbon twirling, high bars, and floor work in her chair, and out of it. There is a very nasty teenage girl who is continuously picking on her, and ruining her selfesteem, the last few weeks she has ramped up the bullying, and she has been trying to tip her out of her wheelchair, twice she has spilt sticky soft drink all over her, and just yesterday while the little girl was standing at the bars, she purposely knocked her on to the ground. Almost breaking her leg." "I'm all over it," I said.

Andy showed me how to, 'feel' the house, so I could pin point exactly where the child was. Then she showed me how to magic a doorway. She used a stick, and drew a rectangle shape, blew glitter on it and viola a doorway.

I have to admit, it was pretty impressive.

The little girl was sitting in the middle of her bed, watching Andy and I. She had tears in her eyes. Hanging on a chair beside her bed was a tiny little pink leotard. I walked up to her and put my hand on her shoulder, her name was Anna she was five years old. And she was born with a condition called Arthrogryposis, but it only affected her legs. Part of her treatment was learning to use and stretch her legs, and that's where the gymnastic lessons came in. She loved the sport, but admitted sometimes it was hard, and her legs hurt for days after. She told me she was going to be a famous gymnast and be in the Olympics someday. While I had my hand on her shoulder, I could see in her mind. She showed me the elder girl bullying her, pushing her over, pulling her hair, throwing drinks and food at her. Calling her names, and making the others at the gymnastic lessons laugh at her.

Seeing this made me very angry. My brother had also suffered some of these cruel taunts.

Andy was in my mind saying, "Joe, you need to calm down, Anna can feel your emotions too, and your anger is upsetting her, she doesn't know why she had made you angry."

I forced myself to calm down, taking deep breaths for a few minutes. "It's ok little one, I'm not angry at you, I am angry with the girl who's been nasty to you," I told her calmly.

The little girl hugged me, and said, "It's not her fault she is so mean, she probably gets bullied too." That statement brought tears to my eyes, the positiveness of this little girl could show some adults a thing or two. I wanted to be that way, from now on I wanted to see the positives, I wanted to be able to see the bad, but to somehow turn it into the good. I wanted to put the all the crap from the past behind me, and move on to a positive happier future.

I whispered the phrase **'Splendor et coruscent facit magicae',** and blew a tiny amount of glitter on the little girls' face.

Andy told me these were ancient magic words used by fairies like us for thousands of years, they helped little kids deal with the hurt and sometimes pain of being bullied, they also soothed them and allowed them to get sleep. But most importantly it sent a beacon out into the universe, which said the bully had been found out, no longer could they hide. The 'Highers', fairies that had gone beyond mentoring who now watched over the mentors and the G M F's (Glitter Magic Fairies), received the signal, and sent punishment to the bully. Andy had told me that sometimes that punishment was death, sometimes a really bad scare, it just depended, on if the Highers thought the bully could be rehabilitated and could mend their ways and become a better person.

The little girl fell into a deep sleep, and she was smiling.

I turned to Andy and gave her a wink. "My work here is done woman, take me home."

Andy smiled, "What was I ever worried about? Of course you're a natural."

I flashed her my brightest smile, the one I used to make girls swoon all over the country.

While flying back home, I had a niggling feeling that Andy may have been responsible for Kevin's improvements. When we got back to my room, I asked Andy, "Did you help Kevin with his pain too?"

"As much as I could, sometimes it didn't seem to be enough though," She replied sadly.

"So, why wasn't the nurse dealt with, buy the Highers?"

"It's not always that easy, I wish for your brother's sake that it was, but because of his age, it made it complicated. I used my glitter and a Highers on him the first time he mind spoke to you. I had to make someone aware of what was happening to him. That nurse was pure evil. And he had to be dealt with. If he had of got away with what he was doing to your brother, he would have got crueller and more monstrous in the years to come, until he turned into one of the evilest nasty things on this planet. Something so sadistic and brutal that none of us want to think about it. I tried several hundred times to make the glitter work on your brother, firstly I tried making him able to talk, but no matter how much we tried he just couldn't form the words that he wanted to. So, then I worked on his hands, hoping that if he could get enough movement in them, he could sign there was a problem. But my magic just wasn't powerful enough for someone his age, in his condition. So, I sent a request to a friend of mine, my mentor actually, Rosemary, she's an elite Higher. I begged and pleaded with her to help so he could at least mind-speak. She knew you were going to turn into a G M F. I believe that's the only reason she eventually agreed to help."

"What about the last time he ESP'd me, was that you too?" I asked.

"No, that's complicated too, I'll do my best to explain. Some times when we are dying, we can throw our 'consciousness' out to the universe, people perceive this as a visit from the spirit world. All too often you hear stories of a loved one visiting family members on the day or night before they die. Some times to say goodbye, or sometimes to relay messages, they never told anyone when they were alive. I think your brother knew he had the stroke, and was dying, so he threw his 'consciousness' at you and said things to you he had wanted to tell you for years. Your brother loved you, from the moment he found out you were coming into his world, he had dreams of things he wanted to show you, teach you. He was going to make sure you were the most spoilt little brother in history. Part of the reason he fought so hard to come to you the last night, was he wanted to make sure you were going to be ok. Towards the end of the conversation, I was there in both your minds. He could feel your love for him pour from you. He knew, Joe, you never have to doubt it."

I was blubbering like a baby now, I couldn't speak. Andy stepped over and hugged me, "It's ok to cry, let it all out, you are becoming an amazing man Joe, and there are some good things coming your way. You have earnt them. But there is also going to be some more shit times, but your strong and you will get through them."

She gently pushed me back and I fell into my bed and she blew glitter on me.

The next morning my eyes were sticky from the dried tears and I had to wash my face before I could open then properly.

Chapter 12

A few weeks later when I was doing my chores, I noticed fresh tyre prints on the track to my stables. They weren't from any of our vehicles. I finished up my chores and knocked on dads' study door. I asked him if everything was ok?

He asked "Why?"

I told him about the tyre tracks, and said, "I though you may have had to get the vet in."

He said, "No."

The driveway gates hadn't been locked in for ever. I told to him, "It might be time to start locking the gates again as my two show horses were starting to make a name for themselves here, and overseas and I wasn't ready to risk their safety or that of the other horses we had on the property over an unlocked gate."

He agreed and said, "He would get a lock smith in to check the gate locks over and make sure they were ok."

"The sooner the better," I said, the tyre tracks had spooked me a bit and I had a strange feeling it meant trouble.

I took Molly for a ride around the property, and checked all the fences, perimeter and paddock, everything looked ok, but still I had a strange feeling in the pit of my stomach. We currently had thirty-five horses on the property, ten of those new

Foals, worth somewhere around the five-million-dollar figure.

I had been offered almost that much alone, for Harry recently. They were my two unique horses, but also one of dads two-year-old filly's, the new bred we had been working on, the Arabian cross quarter horse, won a prestigious horse race a couple months ago, and now everyone wanted one of our horses.

We had been really lax with our security efforts as of late. It was time to step it up.

Every day I had mind conversations with Andy, I told her things about the horses and the farm, she kept teaching me about being a G M F. She told me about the Osines that wanted to steal our glitter, and ultimately wanted all G M F's dead. They were exceptionally strong, and it took a few G M F's to bring them down, if a G M F encountered an Osine when they were on their own. If the G M F was lucky then they might be able stun the Osine long enough to escape. She said, "They had a tiny little bit of their own magic, which they used to glamour themselves so normal humans would befriend them. If humans saw them the way we did, all the humans would run for the hills. Thankfully there wasn't many of them around. The Osine order was Youngling, they were just newly venturing into the world as an Osine, they were very weak and could be easily over powered by a couple of G M F's. They could be any age from late teens to ninety. They rarely travelled alone, usually always accompanied by at least one normal Osine.

Normal Osines, or just Osines were the next highest level, they were incredibly strong, but really stupid. They like to tell lies, and in fact most of what they say is lies, they smell really bad, and some of the more magically minded G M F's say they feel like ice, or they claim the temperature plummets whenever one is around. Some have learnt the art of mind-speak, but they are not good at it, they get easily confused, and can only concentrate on prominent thoughts, they can't dig deeper into the mind. They are like you Joe, normal G M F's, but G M F's are way more resourceful, and we have glitter and can fly. But G M F's are nowhere near as strong as an Osine. An Osine can over power a lone G M F in seconds. Then there are elder Osines, these are the tricky ones, they have used the glamour for so long it has become part of them, they are very hard to distinguish from normal humans. They are hugely powerful, and it takes Highers, mentors and G M F's to bring them down, they are evil personified. They will kill any fairy that gets in their way. Oh, and they have poison in their fingernails, that will kill a G M F in hours. Any part of their skin that's exposed to air contains a slippery acid, that not only makes it impossible to grab them, but eats away at a fairy's skin. It has been said that there are some fairies, whom the acid doesn't really react to other then a slight irritation. Although I have never met a G M F that is that magically powerful. Our glitter can supposedly help to calm the acid from their limbs, so in theory I would imagine that glitter from a couple of us would almost neutralize it, but that's unproven. Even fairies that are magically strong cannot take on an elder Osine, and survive. Somewhere in between an Osine and an elder Osine is a transformer, one who is just about to make the change. But to an untrained eye, they would just look like a normal Osine, except they would be stronger if engaged in combat. They can be extra powerful."

She went on to warn me about never giving an Osine permission to use the glitter, as that would cause catastrophic consequences, and could lead to the destruction of the whole world. She also informed me that Osines had a built-in code, and they could never harm a normal human, they could threaten to, and they could capture one, but they couldn't ever actually hurt one. But they can use their glamour to make humans do their bidding, so in theory they could force a human to kill another human for them.

"Oh nice," I said sarcastically.

Chapter 13

A week later I was off with Andy on another rescue. This time we were heading to the city. As we got close, two other fairies joined us. Rex and Amelia they introduced themselves as.

Rex was a bit shorter than I was, he had surfer blonde hair, bright orange eyes and in the city lights his wings were dark blue with gold flecks.

Amelia was taller than him, she had a stocky build, drop dead gorgeous looks, silver eyes and her wings were silver with purple glittery splatters. "How's it going?" I offered in greeting to them.

"I see you are a natural flyer," Rex said via mind-speak, "Took me weeks to figure it out. I had a little bird to focus on and if I got distracted, bang I hit the ground. And when Ams here joined our little team, I was always distracted. I lost count of the amount of times Andy had to rescue me."

Amelia said in my mind, "He got so banged up I started refusing to come on missions. I was so scared he was going to get seriously hurt."

"The only thing that was hurting me, was you ignoring babe," Rex replied.

"I was shy." she replied sheepishly.

Andy cut in and said, "We all good now? Can we continue with the rescue?"

"Sure," I replied. And I flashed my 100-watt smile into her mind.

I heard her sigh.

Amelia giggled, "Oh yeah you're definitely trouble boyo."

We landed on top of a block of apartments, about thirty stories high.

All serious now, Andy said, "Joe I want you to find the apartment we are needed in."

"Can do," I said, I flew around the building, one level at a time. I knew exactly where I needed to be as soon as we go close to the building, but I loved this flying thing and I did not want to seem cocky around my new colleagues.

The twenty-third floor is where we needed to be. Apartment number ninety-two. That apartment dripped sadness. I returned to the others and told them where we were needed.

"Very good," Andy said, "But you could have just mind spoke us the details."

"Were would the fun be in that?" I replied cheekily.

Rex pulled a short piece of steel out of the waist band of his jeans and it had a rubber knob on one end. He saw me looking at it and he said, "The gear stick from the car my brother was killed in. He was a racing car driver."

"I'm so very sorry," I said.

"He died doing something he was passionate about, if only we could all be that lucky," he replied."

He made a doorway straight into the side of the building with the gear stick and we entered a set of children's rooms, which included a huge play area. There were three bedrooms that led off the playroom. Rex and Amelia took a room each and Andy and I took the other room. A little baby about eight months old was sitting in a cot in the middle of the room.

I looked at Andy "How is this going to work?" I ESP'd her."

"You'll see," she replied.

I walked up to him and put my hand through the bars on the cot and on to his shoulder.

He was burbling away in baby language. As soon as my hand touched his shoulder, I found out his name was Eli, and he was eight and a half months old. Him and his older brother and sister went to a day care centre at the bottom of the building. There were heaps of kids at the centre, too many for the few careers to look after and they wouldn't put more staff on because they were being greedy, I guessed.

"Yes!" Andy said to my mind.

The staff couldn't supervise all the children plus all the other staff. One of the staff members had started bullying the kids. Whenever she was alone with them, she would smack them for no reason, hard enough to leave bruises. The babies she waited until she was changing their nappies then she would belt them hard on their bare bottoms. Enough that a hand print was left on the skin. The baby would cry, then she would smack it again and tell it to shut up. The toddlers would get similar treatment. The elder kids would get their legs slapped or she would punch their little arms. If a child she was looking after cried, she removed their lunch, and wouldn't let them eat it. She made them sit and watch the other kids eating. When the parents came to pick the children up, most of the marks had faded, she was careful not to do the smacking late in the afternoon. She would tell the parents of the child that they had not been hungry today, and that's why they hadn't eaten anything.

I whispered the phase to the little baby '**Splendor et coruscent facit magicae'.** He tumbled over sideways, stuck his thumb in his mouth and was sound asleep. I gently pulled the covers over him.

We all met up back on top of the building. "I hope the bitch gets what she deserves," I said.

Everyone agreed.

"I'm sure she will," Andy told us.

Chapter 14

I just turned nineteen and life was getting better. I still missed my brother every single day, but most days I remembered all the good stuff, and not so much of the bad. I had a steady girl friend who I thought lots of, did I love her? No probably not. But I loved when we were together. She was into horses, and that's where we met, at a horse show. She loved the outdoors and roughing it. Her family owned a chain of super markets. So, she wasn't with me for my money. More about the way my butt filled my jeans.

Andy was still my number one girl though and I talked to her about anything and everything.

About six weeks after my birthday, I went out early one morning to get my chores done and I was going to put some time into saddle breaking Harry. It was time the lazy little sod did some hard work. He now stood at 22 hands high and he was at least two of me wide across his shoulders. Because I worked him on the lunge rein daily for a couple hours each time, his muscles rippled. I went as usual to Molly's stall in my stables first. She was gone!! The outer gate from her stall, that led to the paddock, was open. I had a bit of a chuckle, it wasn't the first time she had decided to let herself out. Too smart for her own good that horse. I walked to her paddock and whistled for her. There was no answering nicker. I waited a few minutes and then whistled again, louder this time. Still there was no reply, and she wasn't running across the paddock either.

There was no sign of her. Some of the other mares were out as well. I thought that was odd, she had never let any of the other horses out before.

They were standing at the opposite edge of the paddock under some branches that hung over from an open area. It wasn't fenced but it had an amazing little grove of trees with a clearing in the middle. I walked over to the mares and even stranger still, they had been mixed up, some were mine, and some were dads. I searched for Molly, but she wasn't anywhere, I grabbed one of the other mares by the mane and swung up on her back, this paddock was too big to search by foot. I kicked her into a canter, while calling for Molly the whole time. There was no sign of her. As we neared the front of the property, I could see the fence had been smashed and there were fresh tyre prints. They were the same as the ones I had found last year. I couldn't believe what I was seeing. Where the hell was my mare? I pushed the one I was on to jump the pile of smashed fence. As soon as we were free of debris I kicked her into a gallop. I was now frantic. I searched the whole property, the first stop was Harry's pen, but she wasn't there and neither was Harry. I kicked the mare to go faster and headed her towards the house. I galloped her on to the veranda and slid off her at the first sliding door I came to. Dad came out to abuse me for galloping the mare so close the house but the look on my face must have said it all. He grabbed me by the shoulders, "Son what's wrong?" he demanded.

"THEY'RE GONE!" I shouted.

"Joe, settle down please, you need to calmly talk to me," dad answered.

Andy was in my brain saying, "Joe, breathe, calm down before you hurt someone."

"I'll kill the bastard that took my horses," I growled via mind-speak.

"Dad, someone's taken Molly and Harry," I said as calmly as I was able to. "The fence has been smashed and the locks on the main gate have been cut."

Dad went to the phone and called the police, then he called every vet in a three-hour radius and described the horses and told them the brand they should be looking for.

The police arrived as dad finished talking to the last vet. That's what happens when you provide their service horses.

The police called in investigators, and detectives. The horses couldn't be sold, they were too distinct, and they would be recognised immediately both here and overseas. Only problem was, if they got overseas, I would never get them back.

I was a failure. I couldn't keep my brother safe and I couldn't keep my horses safe either. I broke down into tears.

What business did I have trying to keep kids safe.

The police asked twenty-thousand questions and I was getting aggravated with them.

"JUST GO FIND MY DAMN HORSES!" I yelled at them.

"We will find them" a detective told me, "But we need as much info as you can give us."

He asked what the market value of the horses was. I told him about twenty million. They were unique, Harry was still a young horse but he wasn't gelded so he could be studded. Molly had won so many awards, her colouring was also unique, and she was still of breeding age. I swore and used a word I rarely used "XXXX. I want my horses back!" Just then Aunty Denny came out of her room and she put her arms around me.

"Joe please calm down," she said, "Remember what I told you about bad language."

I bit my lip so hard blood started running down my chin.

"Who would take my horses?" I asked nobody.

I told the detective about the last lot of those exact tyre tracks, just weeks after Kevin died. Dad went out and was about to take the mare I was riding back to her stall. He called to me as he was closing the screen door.

"Joe, out here. We have a fence to fix and horses to sort."

"I'll take her," I said to him. I swung back up on the mare's back and gently cantered her back to the stables. I locked her back in her stall, then went into the paddock and called my other mares over, I locked them all up, with extra hay.

Of course, dad's mares weren't trained to come when they were called so we had to go get them. I jumped on one of them, and we herded the others through the broken fence and into their own paddock, then to their own stalls. I slipped of the mare and locked her up too. Dad went to his stallions' stalls, they were all there. He turned to me and asked, "Were any of my fences down?" I shook my head.

"So, someone had let mine out, and put them in with yours?" he enquired.

"Looks that way," I mumbled.

"Joe, I know your angry and pissed right now, and you have absolutely every right to be but at this moment, we have to let the police do their job. You will get them back, I promise, but we have a whole team of other horses to protect and that means we have to get the fences fixed and better locks installed. I have already called the lock smith and he is on his way."

I nodded and mumbled in agreement because I knew he was right. Everything had to be secured for when I got them back.

We finished fixing the fences. The lock smith was installing a three-way security system with security cameras everywhere.

I walked inside to check the horse sales on the laptop, in case anyone was stupid enough to try and sell them there.

I had emails waiting and I nearly didn't read them, but I clicked them absentmindedly.

One email was marked as urgent, but I didn't recognise the sender. I opened it and the email was a ransom note! I rushed out to the detective that was still in the stables. He came into my office, and copied the email and send it to himself. The kidnappers wanted five million dollars, by tomorrow night, or my babies would be sold to an overseas buyer and I would never see them again. The detective made a couple of phone calls, he said there would be a computer expert here tonight. The detective started to laugh.

 "What's so funny?" I asked.

"By sending an email they have ensured their speedy capture," he said. "Our techies will have a name and address within hours and buy this time tomorrow, your horses will be safely back in their pens." He promised.

"I'll hold you to that," I told him.

"You can bank on it," he stated.

Chapter 15

That night I tossed and turned and couldn't get to sleep. When I felt Andy's presence in my room, I was wide awake.

"Tonight? Of all nights?" I said to her.

"Afraid so. I am not sorry though. Joe, you need a distraction from everything that's happened today." she said.

We were flying through the sky. There was a storm brewing out west and it kind of matched my mood.

"What's eating you?" Rex asked.

Before I could answer and rip his head off, Andy replied, "Joes had a rough day, let's just leave it at that, ok?"

"Joe," she said to me, "If you don't calm down, I will fly you back to your house and rip your wings from you. These little kids need you tonight and you need to learn to separate your personal life from the job. So, either your mood temporarily improves or you're no longer a G M F."

I slipped to the back of the formation, took a few deep breaths, glittered myself and cleared my mind, it wasn't easy. Every time I closed my eyes I saw Kevin standing beside Harry, both of them looking at me, accusing me.

"That's only your perception, no one else thinks that Joe," Andy cut in.

I got myself under control, seconds before we landed. I didn't even have a clue where we were. I was focused on controlling myself and wasn't watching where we went. I was just following my built in Radar that told me where I needed to be.

It was an older style farmhouse, like mine but timber. There was an orchard right next to the house and the apple trees were full of ripe red apples.

"On the way out," Andy told us.

We all laughed.

We silently crept up the veranda steps and there was a huge Labrador dog on the top step looking at us.

"It won't hurt you," she said, "Dogs can sense we are not a threat and I have never known of a dog being nasty to a Fairy."

I patted its head as we walked past and it licked my hand and then followed me.

"Good job, you now have a friend for life," Amelia said giggling.

Amelia made our doorway this time. She had stick that she had painted purple and glittered.

"It's not special like Rex's, or Andy's, it's just a stick from a Jacaranda tree in my back yard, painted in my mum's favourite colour," she explained when she saw me looking at it.

I nodded.

"So, your pointy stick is special huh?" I said to Andy.

"Yeah, remind me to tell you about it someday" she quipped.

"Count on it," I said.

The doorway opened to the end of a hallway, which had two doors. Andy and Rex took the left one while Amelia and I took the right one. There were two sets of bunks and a little girl sat on the middle of each mattress, four identical little faces looking at us. I motioned for the little girl on the top to sit on the bottom with her sister, while Amelia did the same on her side. I put my hand on the shoulder of the little girl closest to me, she was seven and her name was Karen, her sister was Kay, and on the other bed was Kat and Kylie. WOW, I thought. The little girl showed me the next room where her three identical nine-year-old brothers were. I smiled, someday that's what I wanted, a pile of kids.

"Does your partner get a say in that?" Amelia asked.

"The right girl for me, will want what I do," I told her.

"Uh huh," she replied.

Andy interrupted, "Are you two working tonight?"

"Sure are," I replied. And sent her my 100-watt smile as an image in her mind

She sighed.

Karen proceeded to show me, two sixteen-year-old boys who caught the same school bus they did. The boys were the stereo typical bullies, both over weight, both spoilt rotten, both with amazing home lives and parents who doted on them. They weren't brothers and were actually not related, all though they looked the same. They took food from the girls, pulled their hair, pushed them over, stole tuck shop money out of their bags, teased them because their skin colour was different, all the normal bully things. When their brothers tried to stick up for them, the two older boys beat the little boys up, pretty badly, leaving them with black eyes, bruises and ripped uniforms. The parents being only new to the country did not know what to do. Luckily, we did.

I lifted the little girl back to her own bed and held my hands out and both girls held a hand each. I whispered the words **'Splendor et coruscent facit magicae'** and they were both fast asleep. I pulled their covers over them and waited for Amelia to finish, then we headed out to the hallway, where Andy and Rex were waiting for us.

We went back through the doorway and Amelia closed it. The dog was waiting patiently for us. I patted him again on our way down the stairs. After filling our pockets and mouths with fresh sweet juicy apples, we all flew off as one, into the night sky. We didn't go straight home though, we stopped in a little park in a tiny little town. We sat at a picnic table. Rex And Amelia told Andy they had decided it was time.

I looked at Andy, and said "Umm time for what?"

Rex and Amelia are leaving the G M F family to go and start a family of their own. Andy explained.

"Ohhh," I said, "Can't we have both?"

"Usually not," Andy replied curtly.

"Ok well then I wish you both all the best," I said.

"So, it will just be me and you," I said to Andy.

"Just for a while yes, we will have a new fairy very soon," she stated.

"Now Joe," Andy said, "Do you think you can make your own way home? Rex and Amelia would like this done ASAP and I made an appointment to meet Rosemary at their place, now actually." Looking down at an imaginary watch on her arm.

"Sure thing," I told her.

"Great I will catch up with you tomorrow," she answered.

I hugged Rex and Amelia awkwardly. I hadn't really known them that long and they kept their thoughts pretty much to themselves and they rarely shared very much wisdom with me. I vowed that I wouldn't be like that with the new G M F, I would shower them with info and my thoughts.

Andy and the others left, I waited all of a split second before I left too. I was going to go on a little hunting mission. I was pretty sure that if I flew over my horses, I would know they were there, and I could rescue them.

Andy butted in, "NO! Joe too many opportunities for things to go wrong. How would you explain to the police how you found the horses? That's just for starters, if you were caught trespassing on some one's land, regardless of why you were there, you could end up in jail. With these two leaving, I need you Joe, the kids need you."

I sighed, "Yeah ok point made, I'll just go home and do nothing while my babies are being subjected to who knows what."

I very sadly flew home. I had to enter my end of the house with my spare key, as I did not know yet how to make a doorway. I'd seen it done and it looked easy enough but I wasn't up for trying it tonight. It was late and I was exhausted. I just needed to sleep. I took the two apples that were left from my pockets, they were for my babies when I got them home.

The phone went off early the next morning, dad beat me to answering it by a fingers' length. I only heard his side of the conversation. "Yes, ok, I understand, we will be there soon." "Well?" I asked.

"They have found them," dad said.

I fell to the ground, the relief flooded through me. "Wait, are they ok? Are they hurt? Where are they?" I fired at dad.

"Andy, Andy?" I called in ESP, "They found them, they found them!"

"Joe, I am so happy for you," Andy replied and she sent me a mind pic of her smiling.

Dad continued, "They're ok and they have taken them to the vet to get them checked over just for.....precautions. We are going to head off to the police station, to see if you want to lay charges."

"What aren't you telling me? Dad! What's wrong with my horses," I demanded. I could feel something wasn't right and I was getting more agitated at what he wasn't telling me, as the seconds ticked by.

"Joe, just calm down please," he replied.

"No, I won't calm down. What the hell is wrong with my horses?" I yelled.
Dad sighed, "Molly is ok, but has some pretty bad lacerations from a whip, nothing that won't heal in time. Harry isn't doing so well and the vet can't get close enough to him to check him over."

I was running for my ute, my legs wouldn't go fast enough, my hands were balled into fists. "Of course, I want whoever did this charged," I spat at dad.

"We will see," dad said mysteriously.

Chapter 16

My ute that dad was driving hadn't even stopped before I opened the door and got out, at the vets. I raced inside nearly knocking into an elderly man with a fluff ball coming the other way. I stopped long enough to say I was sorry, then kept rushing inside. The receptionist knew who I was as we had dated a couple times. She pointed me towards the back of the building. My horses were in a large concrete and brick room. Harry was tied to a hitch down on the other side of room. The vet was checking Molly over when I went in. He looked up at the exact same time I saw the whip marks all over her back and legs.

"Now Joe, calm down, it looks bad, but.... **Joe!**" the vet tried to get my attention.

I was ignoring him. I walked up to my baby, and gently rubbed her neck. Some of the whip marks were so deep. She turned her head and licked my face. Whoever did this to you will pay and they will pay severely I promised her. I walked over to Harry, my blood was boiling. Someone was going to die today. Andy kept trying to pop into my head but I pushed her out and closed down the connection. (Yes, I know that was against the rules, yes, I know I could lose my wings, but right now I don't care). Harry shied away and tried to break his lead. His eyes were wild, and he was scared. He pawed the ground and was throwing his head wildly from side to side, he was raring and then falling hard on his front hooves, his nostrils were flaring and he was snorting out a warning to me to stay away. I looked at my big beautiful stallion, he was never going to be the same again. He would always be wary of people now. It was going to take months of rehabilitation for me to be able to even get close to him again. I swore. I left the building, went around to my ute, got in the passenger's side and commanded dad to drive to the police station. He had parked the float while I was in seeing my horses and had left it out the back of the vets. He drove out of the vets and pulled up on the side of the road.

He turned to look at me, "Joe you need to settle down, if you hurt anyone you will go to jail son. I know those horses are your world, believe me I do. But I can't run the horse stud without you there buddy."

"**Drive**," I ground out through clenched teeth. I had one hand balled into a fist and I was punching my other hand with it. I was like high tensile wire and was about to snap.

When we pulled up at the police station, I reached behind the seat of my ute, and pulled out my 6foot, 180 cm whip and tucked it into my jeans waist band.

"Joe, **JOE**, you can't," Dad said, and tried blocking my way. I pushed him to the side, and strode into the police station. The detective working the case saw me. He came over and was about to engage in pleasantries until I cut him off and said, "Where is he?" He pointed to a room, but said to me," You can't go in there."

I strode past him, kicked opened the door and then when I was inside I locked it. I even blew glitter on it to make absolutely sure no one could get in, unless I let them.

Sitting inside was a stocky forty something year old man, wearing a black dusty cowboy hat, faded blue jeans and a checked faded long sleeve shirt. He still had his riding boots on, and spurs were attached to them. I walked up to him and grabbed him by the shirt and I pulled him to his feet, lifting his feet off the ground so he was eye level with me.

I got right up in his face and said to him, "For your sake I hope you did not touch my horses with those spurs? If I find out you have, then if you don't die from what I am about to do to you, I will find you and finish the job. You like to hit innocent animals with whips huh."

He started to shake.

"Weak pathetic P O S." I growled at him. I dropped him on his feet and took a couple of steps back I pulled my whip from my belt.

"Let's see how you like it," I snarled. I released the whip so it grabbed him around his waist, he screamed out in pain.

"Hurts, huh," I said. I pulled it back and hit him with it again, this time around his legs. I flicked it hard enough to cut his skin, but because of his jeans it didn't do any damage. Then I flicked the tail of it across his face and left a deep cut on his cheeks. I then hit his back with it about three times. He was screaming and crying in pain.

"Now you know what my horses went through." I was just about to hit him again, when I was grabbed and restrained by two officers. I looked at the guy who was now bleeding, he had peed his pants.

I laughed at him and tried to kick the daylights out of him. I only got a couple in when the two officers restraining me pulled me further away, so as the scum was out of my reach.

Another officer removed the guy from the room, making sure he kept him well and truly away from me. The detective came in and slammed the door shut behind him.

"Just what the hell do you think you were doing?" he yelled at me, "I should damn well throw the book at you and lock you up in the cell beside his!"

"DID YOU SEE THE CONDITION OF MY HORSES? DO YOU KNOW WHAT IT'S GOING TO TAKE TO MAKE HARRY TRUST ME ENOUGH TO LET ME NEAR HIM AGAIN? I WILL NEVER BE ABLE TO SHOW HIM AGAIN, HE WILL ALWAYS BE TOO SKITTISH AROUND PEOPLE NOW!" I screamed at the detective. "So, you want to lock me up, GO RIGHT AHEAD, but I advise you not to put me anywhere near his cell, because I will find a way to kill him."

The detective sighed, and rubbed his head. "Joe he wasn't working alone. He was promised one million dollars to do the job."

"So where is the person he was working with? Take me to them NOW," I demanded.

Dad knocked on the door and the officer standing at the door let him in.

He walked up to me and clipped the back of my head. "Do you know how much that little stunt you just pulled cost me? Maybe I should have let you cool off in jail?"

I shrugged. "Its only money, I'll pay it back to you."

"Not the point," he snarled, giving me a piercing stare, and you know it.

The detective said, "I will take you to another room where the master mind to the kidnapping is, but Joe, first you **will** give me your word, she will remain unharmed, or I will handcuff you now, and drag your arse to a cell."

"She?" I asked.

"Yes Joe, she," he replied. "Your word?"

"Yeah righto," I mumbled, my temper nowhere near under control.

He led us to another room, when we entered the room, I looked up and saw my mother seated at a table.

"What the hell is she doing here?" I growled.

Dad walked over and put his hand on my shoulder, "Joe you gave your word" he reminded me sternly.

I looked at her and realised she had handcuffs on. "Somebody had better tell me what's going on here?" I asked, starting to get fired up again.

The detective looked at my mother, "Do you want to tell your son, your only damn living son, for pities sake, why you are in my police station wearing a set of handcuffs?"

She shook her head.

"Ok fine, then I will," the detective said to her.

He began, "Your mother was the one behind the kidnapping. She hired the thug you just beat up, promised him a million bucks to steal your horses and was planning on making a tidy profit from the ransom money for herself."

I sat there with my mouth open in shock, "Andy," I opened my mind again.

"Yes, Joe, I am here. I don't know what you have done, but I just had Rosemary yelling at me, so I guess you are in a lot of trouble," she replied via mind-speak. It was Rosemary who unlocked the door for the police officers."

"It was my mother, she stole my horses."

"I know Joe," she sighed.

"**WHAT?** You knew and didn't think you should share it with me! **Why**?" I gritted out accusingly at her.

"DO NOT take that tone with me. I am still your superior, although I am not sure for how long. But damn Joe, yes, I knew, but if I had told you would you have believed me?" Andy reprimanded sternly.

I sat quietly for a few minutes, thinking about what Andy said. Would I have believed her? Would anyone believe their mother would set a plot in motion to steal what they knew was most precious to one of their kids?

"No, I wouldn't have," I finally replied to her.

I realized the room had been quiet for about ten minutes. I looked at my mother and said "Why?"

She did not reply. I looked at her again and said, "**Why damn it?** I have possibly lost everything in the world that means anything to me today. YOU OWE ME AN EXPLANATION YOU BITCH."

I was struggling to keep the tears away. I had blown my G M F chances, I knew. My horses had been subjected to cruelty like they should have never known. I beat the shit out of a guy with a whip, yeah, he deserved it and right now, right at this moment, I wanted to reach across this table and drive my mother's head into the desk, for causing me so much pain,

and not giving me a reason why.

I stared at her for what seemed like hours. Eventually, she said, "Because you took away everything, I had Joe, the money, my freedom, my lifestyle and my lover."

"What the hell, your lover, the nurse? That one that WAS ABUSING YOUR SON HORRIFICALLY," I screamed at her.

Dad cut in and told her, "No Wendy. You did those things to yourself, none of that was Joes fault. The accident changed you. You were not the same person coming out of it as going into it. Don't blame Joe for your mistakes."

I added, "You're supposed to be my mother, but after the accident you never loved or nurtured me. I needed my mother, but where were you? Kevin needed you too, but no, you were too busy rolling in the hay with a monster."

"You, told your father I was with him. It's your fault. I would have just kept on having it all if it wasn't for you and I wanted to hurt you, bad like your betrayal hurt me," She sneered at me.

I stared at her blankly.

"The money Joe, it's always been about the money. You will never understand how hard it is to survive without money. I have to buy my clothes at commoner shops. Do you know how degrading that is? So yes, I took your precious horses, they weren't supposed to get hurt, the guy said he had experience with horses and floats. By the time I realised he didn't, it was too late. I just wanted you to suffer, I wanted you to hurt more then you ever had, and I needed the money. I couldn't keep living the way I have been since your father kicked me out," she stated.

I had no words. I **was** hurting deep inside, where I never knew it could hurt. My own mother. I got up to leave and at the door I turned to the detective and said, "Throw the book at her. Every single little charge you can think of, make her wear it. Hell, make some charges up, I don't care. Just keep her locked up for a *very* long time.'"

I left the police station. I wasn't going to wait for dad, he would know where I went. My stomach was turning in knots, I felt like I was going to throw up. I started walking. I still couldn't believe she had done that too me.

"Andy!" I called out in my mind, "Please talk to me. I am so sorry." I felt the tears I had been holding back, now come as a full flood. I tried to control them, but they just kept coming. I slumped on a council chair outside a shop. I was at the lowest point I had ever been. I made a mess of everything, I had let my anger get the best of me. And now, now what?

"Andy," I tried calling her again, breaking down into huge sobs. I was having trouble even trying to mind-speak the words. My ute pulled up on the curb in front of me.

"Get in," dad said.

Chapter 17

I did, we drove to the vets in silence as I couldn't speak. I was still crying my eyes out. My babies were still in the holding paddock behind the vets and I went to them. Dad went to fix the bill up. We had to pay it because the other parties didn't have the funds to do it. I walked to the gate and Molly came up to me straight away. Her wounds had been treated, but she still looked a mess. I wrapped my arms around her warm neck and just held her, tears still pouring uncontrollably from my eyes. She nuzzled her head into my back. I am so sorry I told her, I let you down, I let everybody down.

Andy's voice into my head, "Joe you haven't let anybody down."

I was so pleased to hear her voice, if I wasn't feeling so crappy I would have whooped for joy and sent her a mind pic of my 100-watt smile. But I couldn't summon it.

I stepped away from Molly and tried to walk up to Harry. He kept moving away and if I got to close, his eyes went wild, rolled around in his head until just the white was visible and he started to paw the ground. I held my hands up and said "Ok buddy," then stepped back wards. I sat in the middle of the paddock defeated. Molly came over and rested her head on my shoulder and knelt down with me.

Dad came to the fence, and said, "Joe we have to load the horses now and head home."

"I can't," I told him. "Harry won't go on the float and I can't ride him." I said feeling very close to breaking point. I was scared for my horses, and I felt hopeless and not able to help them. I was also feeling betrayed and let down, I couldn't believe my OWN mother would do something like this to me. I mean I had had no contact with her at all since Kevin's funeral, she never rung me, or emailed, no sms to ask how I was, nothing. I get that she was angry at me, but I guess I don't understand how she could still be blaming me, for what SHE did wrong.

"What do you mean?" dad said.

"He's scared, he won't let me near him. He has really had a bad time of it," I said a new flow of tears and sobs starting.

Dad came into the yard and he walked up to me. Molly neighed, and got up and moved away, "Come on son" he said and held his hand out to help me up.

I took his hand and he pulled me into a hug. We stood there like that for ages. Molly came and put her head on my shoulder too.

He let me go, "Let's see if we can get that horse of yours onto the float," he said.

I shook my head. I tried walking up to Harry again and he backed away so far that his rear end hit the bar at the back of the paddock. He stood up on his back legs and wildly thrashed his front legs in the air.

"Ok, ok, buddy," I said as calmly as I could, and I backed away.

He dropped down to four hooves on the ground again.

Dad said, "I see what you mean. Maybe if we put Molly on, he will go on?"

"It's worth a try," I said doubtfully.

I walked up to Molly and held her halter. Time to go my princess I told her. She turned and licked my face. I nuzzled my face into hers. When dad had the float back on the ute and lined up, I opened the gate, and as I was about to walk through the gate with her, Harry made a run for it and bolted toward the open gate. Without thinking, I stepped in front of him, and waved my hands to stop him escaping. Dad saw what was happening, and raced from the back of the float. The next thing someone pushed me out of the way and then a flash of light and Andy was in the gateway. She was holding her hands up and gently blowing glitter in Harry's direction. He hit the skids, and was trying his best to slow down, but from full bolt it was going to take more room than what was left was between him and Andy. When he was just metres away from slamming into her, he suddenly turned, nearly ended up on the fence, but managed to right himself just in time. He slowed and came to a complete stop at the edge of the paddock. I breathed a sigh of relief that Andy wasn't hurt. Harry was still in the pen, and dad had molly under control. Right at this moment though

I wasn't sure how I was going to explain Andy to dad, I was just glad everyone was ok. I lifted myself out of the dirt and dusted my pants off and closed the gate.

"What the hell happened then?" dad exclaimed. "You know better than to put yourself in front of a bolting scared horse. Have I taught you nothing, boy? He could have killed you. I think the only thing that saved you must have been the fact that you tripped over, and the suddenness of that happening made him slow down, and try to stop. I think he realised he did not want to hurt you. Thankfully."

Andy in my mind, "He did not see me, relax, all he saw was you tripping over."

"If I could right now, I'd hug you to death," I told her.

"Um thanks?" she laughed. "Joe later, when all this is done and dusted you have to tell me what happened when you blocked me out, you're not in the clear yet, not even close, and we have to sort this mess out."

"I know," I sighed.

Before we put Molly on the float I went back into the vets, and got her a light cotton rug. She had a heap of show ones at home, but I wanted one to keep the flies and dust out of her wounds. I didn't know what ailments, germs or diseases would be floating around in this paddock. I put it on her, then we loaded her.

She went on the float with minimal problems.

Harry was standing in the yard watching us the whole time. Andy urged me to try him again, "Use your glitter if you need to," she told me. "Just do it discretely because he can't stay here and if he has to be bribed to get him on that float, then that's what we will do.

I tried walking up to him again and he stood his ground, pawing the dirt, and shaking his head. I sighed and dropped to my knees in front of him. "Back to horse training basics 101," I said to myself. I sat there for ages. Slowly he stopped pawing the dirt. He took a tentative step towards me and reached out his neck to smell me. He jumped back, and stood there. I could see he was unsure. I felt Andy's presence beside me.

"You're going to be here all day," she mind spoke to me. "And there is a storm coming."

"I am trying to regain a little of his trust, he is so scared and I don't want to stress him out more," I said matter of factly.

"I know," she said understandingly.

She held out her hand and the big stallion stretched out his neck again to smell it and as he did she very lightly blew a pile of glitter over his muzzle. The big horse walked forward and nuzzled her hand. I looked at her.

"Show off" I said.

She winked at me, "Now you try."

I did what she had done and Harry rubbed his face all over my hand. I slowly stood up and he didn't flinch. I gently blew more glitter over him. He let me reach up and grab his halter, only prancing around a bit when I had the halter, and him under some sort of control. Andy went to the other side of him and kept blowing glitter on him, while we got him loaded. He reared up as soon as he realised he was going onto the float and he came down really hard, and nearly broke the ramp.

"Are you ok?" I asked Andy. She had glittered herself so no one could see her.

"I'm ok," she said.

We both worked on calming the stallion down with our glitter. Eventually we got him in the float beside his mother. Andy stayed in the float to keep him calm on the way back to the property.

She ESP'd me on the way home, "It doesn't fix the problem Joe, only time and hard work will."

"I know. I will just be happy to have them both back home," I replied.

"Joe, you have a lot of explaining to do, to the Highers, especially Rosemary. She really stuck her neck out for your bother, because she had my word that you would be an asset to the G M F guild. Now it looks like we were all wrong about you. You have no control on that temper of yours and we can't have a loose cannon on the team."

I didn't reply, I had nothing to say. What she said was right. I had messed up too many times.

I hung my head in shame.

Chapter 18

We unloaded the horses at home. We took Molly off first and ended up having to remove the side partition in the float, and turning Harry around, as no amount of glitter, was getting him to back out. Molly went straight into her stall and laid down.

Andy and I coaxed Harry to his paddock, it seemed to take forever. It was getting dark by the time he was secured. There was sheet lightening in the distance. I triple checked everything was locked up. Andy headed to my room and told me she would wait for me there.

I went via the kitchen where Grandma and Aunty were waiting, Grandma hugged me and handed me a coffee, "I could probably do with something stronger" I said, thinking about the conversation waiting for me in my room. She slapped my butt. Dad and I explained what had happened, leaving out the part about me attacking the guy with my whip. Grandma had some fried chicken cooked for our dinner. I mind spoke to Andy about food, she said she was hungry, so I said I would bring her a plate. I loaded up a serving tray with chicken, fresh bread and salads, and took a bottle of red, and two glasses to my room, eyebrows were raised but nothing was said.

I sat on my bed while Andy sat at the desk. As soon as the meal was finished.

Andy said "Come on let's get this done." She led me out to the little grove of trees near the pool, there was a clearing in the middle It was where I used to light bon fires, and bring Kevin out to sit and watch the fire. The fire pit had wood stacked up ready to go, I quickly build a fire and lit it. It went on the first go. I then moved back and sat on a log that had been chain-sawed to resemble a seat, compliments of me. Andy was sitting opposite, and then I felt the wind from wings, and Rosemary landed and sat beside me.

"Where do we start Joe?" she said.

"I did what had to be done. The bastard beat my horses, one will most likely never recover. What was I supposed to do?" I growled out.

"You knew where they were. You knew who took them. You knew they had been hurt and injured, but you did nothing," I said forcefully.

Andy was telling me to settle down in my mind. I wasn't helping the situation.

"You could have told me where they were. You could have punished them for hurting my horses. Harry….," I started to say, but couldn't because I was crying and sobbing and trying to talk while sobbing, was choking me.

"Joe, you beat a guy up with a whip and I can't let that go unpunished. We were all so sure you were perfect for this calling, but now I don't know," Rosemary remarked shaking her head.

"You also put your mother in jail, your own mother Joe, the person who brought you into this world."

"ARE YOU KIDDING ME? AFTER WHAT SHE DID. AFTER SHE BROKE OUR FAMILY APART. YOUR'RE NOW BLAMING ME. HAVE YOU FORGOTTEN WHAT HER BOYFRIEND WAS DOING TO MY BROTHER?" I screamed, unable to hold my temper in anymore. I couldn't believe what she had said.

I continued, **"She wished my brother had died in the accident. She blamed dad for years. Then after the accident she hated me. But you have a go at me!"**

"In years to come Joe, you are going to regret putting her in jail, time has a way of making us forget," Rosemary stated.

"I will **NEVER** forget what she has done," I said between gritted teeth.

"Joe, if you are going to work with already scared little children, you need to control your temper or you will just make them more scared. I am honestly not sure you are fit to be a Glitter Magic Fairy now. You're not even sorry for what you did to that guy are you?"

I shook my head, "I'm not, no. He's just another bully that finally got what was coming to him."

"That's part of my point Joe, you're just not getting it. It isn't your responsibility to deal out punishment," she explained.

I looked over at Andy and her eyes were pleading with me.

"The man you beat up today has five kids to look after, his wife is terminally ill and he is unable to work, because he has to be at home to watch the kids and care for his wife. The money your mother offered him, was going to help their family immensely," Rosemary continued.

"That did not make it ok for him to beat my horses," I stated defeatedly.

"No, it did not, but Joe the reason it isn't up to you to deal punishment is because that man is in a hospital bed tonight. The wounds from your whip deep and starting to get infected. His children are fending for themselves, his wife is lying alone in a palliative care bed, wondering what she did wrong to stop her family coming to see her today."

I looked at my feet, I couldn't meet her eyes I was so.... Ashamed at how I had behaved. Fresh tears threatened to start again.

"I'm sorry, I didn't know. He hurt my horses. I didn't ... I'm sorry" I apologised.

"Joe," she said, and turned my face to look at hers. "Can you promise me you will work on that temper of yours?"

I was unable to speak, so I nodded.

She reached up and wiped away a tear from my cheek.

"You really are going to be an asset to our family, but you need to learn some control. You are going to come across situations that are going to make you boil from the inside out, but you can't go around whipping everyone who pisses you off. Although we all know life would be easier if we could," she added.

When I had the sobs under some sort of control again I managed to mind-speak.

"I AM so so, very very, sorry. There is nothing I can say. I won't make excuses for my behaviour. It was appalling. All I could see was Harry and Kevin, and I knew I had failed them because I couldn't keep them safe. All I can do is promise you both I will work on my temper. I love being a G M F, please give me another chance, you will never regret it again. Never again will I try to dish out my own punishments, actually I won't even bother myself with the punishment of others. I owe you so much for what you both did for my brother. Please!" I begged both her and Andy.

I could sense that they were both deep in conversation, excluding me.

I got up to put more wood on the fire. Andy said "Joe, sit back down, watch and learn." Andy winked at me.

From where she was sitting, she blew glitter on the fire, suddenly it roared to life, and stayed burning bright and warm, without wood.

"You can't do it without some sort of fire already being there, so there at least has to be hot coals," she explained.

I sat back down next to Rosemary and waited for one of them to say something.

Rosemary spoke up about ten minutes later. "Your behaviour today was nothing short of atrocious, but as it wasn't against the guild and as long as you swear to NEVER repeat it, Andy and I have decided to let you off with a warning. But let me make this perfectly clear young man, **you will not be given another chance, ever!** Learn to use the magic you have been given correctly and most of your problems will be solved." With that, she flew off and vanished into the night sky.

"You are so lucky," Andy replied, "I have seen G M F's stripped of everything, over a lot lessor crimes." I went and hugged Andy.

"You know I love you right?" I said to her, "You're the mum I never really had."

She said, "Yes, I know. That's a big part of a mentor's role, in the lives of their Fairies, to be what the G M F needs."

"Andy," I enquired "What's with the stick?"

"The stick is what we call a focus tool, it helps us to direct our magic and the glitter where we need it to be. For example, when we make a doorway, a focus tool helps us to draw a perfect rectangle, and the tool leaves a groove in the surface we need to open.

It's not a visible groove, you can't walk up and see it. But it's there, and the glitter knows it's there, and is attracted to it, and it forms the seal for the doorway. Does that make sense?" she explained.

"Kinda," I nodded.

"And your stick?" I asked.

"My stick came from a tree my uncle planed many years ago. The timber in the tree was used to make his coffin with. My 'stick' came from the milled timber that was too be used to make the coffin with," Andy replied. "But as you heard from Amelia, not all focus tools need to be special."

"Her's kind of was though," I shrugged.

"What do you mean?" Andy asked.

"Well, it, kind of was part of her home and reminded her of her mother," I stated.

"Yes, I guess you are right when you think about it. You have a very unique and special way of seeing the world sometimes Joe," Andy said.

Andy said, "She had to be going and asked me if I was going to be ok."

I nodded. "I think so."

I have my babies back at least. Although I know I have months of work ahead of me now. Molly was going to recover, it would take time, but at least she still trusted me, and knew I wasn't to blame for what happened. Harry was a whole other kettle of fish though. He didn't trust me anymore, and even if I spent months working to build that trust back up, I'm not sure he would ever trust anyone ever again. I couldn't show a skittish horse. Sitting there thinking about my horses, and how I hadn't been able to protect them, brought a fresh round of tears to my eyes.

Andy's voice in my head saying, "Joe it wasn't your fault, you love those horses and you were prepared to give up everything for them, they really do know that, I promise you Harry does too.

It is just going to take him time."

I sat there for ages after Andy left, just thinking about everything. Watching the fire burn. I could hear whinnying and neighing in the paddocks, the soft calls of mares to their foals. Stallions calling out warnings to predators in the night. I sighed, I really had come very close to losing everything today. I was still in shock learning that my own mother was to blame. I really hoped she rotted in a jail cell. It should have been her that died, not Kevin.

Andy inside my head again, "Unfortunately Joe the world doesn't work like that."

I glittered the fire out, I didn't even wonder how to, it was just natural.

I knew what I was going to do, I had searched Rosemary's mind and found out which hospital the guy I had whipped was staying in. I flew off into the night, making sure I had closed every gap in

my mind, so as no one would be able to reach me, not Andy and definitely not Rosemary.

I found him easy enough, he was having a tough time of it. He was lying uncovered on a hospital bed, when I saw the mess I had made of his body, I hung my head in shame. He was in a deep sleep and I guessed the hospital had given him something to help with the pain and so he could sleep. I glittered myself invisible, then very carefully applied a thin layer of glitter over his body, a slightly thicker layer where his lacerations were. As I was using my glitter, I was repeating over and over again that I was sorry. I searched his mind and found out where he lived. I headed off to his house.

I used glitter to let myself into the house, via the front door, it was nearing morning, and I sensed these little kids had gone to bed hungry because there wasn't anyone here to get them dinner. I felt worse than ever now. My heart was crumbling, it was my fault, I did this. I left the house and found an all-night small goods shop, I brought bacon, eggs, sausages, bread, tomatoes, pancake mix, tiny cereal packets and fresh milk. I took it all back to the house and cooked it all up, while all the children were still sleeping. I used fairy dust to make sure I didn't wake those poor little kids up. I left big piles of cooked food covered in alfoil on the table. I could hear the children starting to stir, so I quickly left via the front door, being extra careful to make sure no-one saw me. I called past the hospital on my way home and the man was making an amazing recovery, to the surprise of the staff, he would be well enough to go home after breakfast.

When I got home I was exhausted. The sun was well and truly up and I was so tired, I could barely keep my eyes open. I pulled my phone out of my pocket and turned it on, then turned the sound off. I had ten missed messages from my steady girlfriend. I sat there staring at the screen, I was really going to have to break it off with this chick because she was too clingy and she wasn't ever going to be the *one*.

 I headed up to my end of the house, but changed my mind and headed to the stables instead. I unlocked the doors, and relocked them from the inside then I walked over to Molly's stall, opened her gate, and went and sat down on her clean bedding. She neighed at me, and licked my face. I told her she was a weird horse and she nuzzled into my chest in answer. I was mentally and physically drained, and shivering from cold. I needed to rest for a few hours so I laid down in the fresh hay. Molly curled herself around me. I warmed up, and using her belly as a pillow I fell asleep.

Chapter 19

A week later Andy and I were off on another rescue. We flew to the northern suburbs of Brisbane to a new housing estate. There was a war going on, on opposite sides of a playground and it was starting to get nasty, as some of the kid's parents were getting involved. The kids in the older houses on one side of the playground, claimed it as theirs, and were refusing to share it with the kids from the new estate. The playground had a skate park in it, and blood had been spilt there yesterday.

A little boy who was pushed off his skate board, and needed twelve stitches, was the one we were here to see.

"By helping him, we would in turn be helping them all," Andy said.

Andy asked me to do the honours with a doorway. I pulled Kevin's magic wand from the waist band of my jeans.

"Very fitting," Andy said, nodding in approval and patting my shoulder.

I magic'd us a rough, but useable doorway and we stepped through. The little boy was sitting on his bed looking at the big bandage on his knee, his bottom lip trembling. I glanced up at Andy and she had a single tear slipping down her cheek. I winked at her.

I very carefully sat beside the little boy so as not to disturb his bed too much and hurt his little knee more. I didn't need him to show me what had been happening, I already knew. I put my hand on his shoulder and whispered **'Splendor et coruscent facit magicae'.** I also gently blew some glitter on his little knee, to help it heal. He fell back into his bed, fast asleep. His lip no longer trembling. We left as silently as we had arrived, I magic'd the doorway closed behind us.

As we were flying home, Andy told me we would be being joined by a new G M F very soon. Her name was Mishie, and she was a real sweetie. She was very easy going, and passionate about the rights and wrongs in life, but she hadn't taken to flying as well as I did. Actually, not one Andy's students ever had. So I needed to give her some time to adjust.

"Her mind-speak is still coming in too, so don't expect to be the centre of her universe for a while." Andy explained. She flashed me a full colour picture of the new recruit. My heart started racing. I broke out in a sweat. I was gasping for breath. I wolf whistled, and for the first time EVER I nearly fell out of the sky.

"Indeed, but I don't think she will approve of your whistling at her," Andy winked at me.

"Of course she will, I haven't meet a chick yet who can resist my charm," I grinned.

I had been working with my horses and most of Molly's wounds had healed. I had been glittering them to help fix them. A couple looked as if they might scar, but I was doing everything I could to try not to let that happen.

Harry's wounds weren't as easy to heal. I had spent hours sitting quietly in his pen, waiting for him to make the first move. He tries, but as soon as he smells human, he shies away. I am trying to have to not use the glitter, I want him to do it on his own. Today I am going to try putting a carrot and an apple in my pockets.

I sat there in his pen for about an hour. He was interested in the fruit I had, as he was creeping forward a little more each time, before shieing away. About another hour later he came close enough to take the carrot from my hand. I did not move, or try to pat him, he had to build confidence and trust up again. Today was a huge win for us both. When he finished the carrot, he trotted off to the other side of the paddock. And I went and did some other chores. I had four new foals born in the last month, one filly was silver. Yes silver, not grey, with flecks that sparkled like glitter.

Two days past, just on dark, I received a message from Andy, she was on her way, and would like us to meet in a park at the Brisbane River. She wanted me to meet the new recruit, but she didn't want the first time I met her to be in a rescue.

"Mishie gets easily distracted, and we don't want to jeopardize rescue missions." Andy explained. I arrived before they did, and sat on a picnic table waiting. I saw them long before they found me. As soon as they entered the park, I noticed a glow, it was the new recruit, she was glowing like a beacon.

"Um hi," I said when they got close to the table I was sitting at.

Andy smiled and said, "Hi yourself, I'd like you to meet Mishie, Mishie this is Joe."

I flashed my 100-watt smile and said "Hello."

This chick was, she was, just, wow.... Drop dead gorgeous, she had short, just below her ear level bright blue hair. The biggest eyes I had ever seen, lilac like Harry's mane and tail. Perfectly pointed ears. She looked like a living breathing pixie. Her Skin shone like pearls, in the light of the moon. Her body was perfectly proportioned and had all the right curves. But it was something else, something coming from with-in her. It was like a strand of white life force that radiated from her. That joined up with my own strands of life. It made me feel like I had known her for longer than I had been alive, but at the same time something new and exciting. My skin tingled with electricity just being near her. I knew instantly she was the one.

"Hi, nice to meet you," she said shyly.

"ANDY I'm dying," I ESP'd to Andy.

She just giggled, "I thought it might be like that, that's why we are meeting here."

I asked Mishie about Thirty thousand questions. Where are you from? How did you get the calling? All the normal stuff. But it still felt as if I was nowhere near knowing anything about her and we talked about everything and nothing until the early hours of the morning. When Andy said it was time to go, I felt like a part of me was being torn away. I flew with them as far as Andy let me, then she shooed me off home. I touched my finger tips to Mishie's as I flew off in the direction of home. That slight touch made my whole-body ache, and my heart beat increase like I had just run a marathon.

The next morning, I woke Andy super early with my mind-speak. I asked if Mishie had said anything about me after they left? When was I going to see her again? Why would Andy do this to me?

"Joe stop," Andy replied, "Sheesh boy let me open my eyes."

"Sorry," I said sheepishly.

"She said and I Quote 'he's nice', that's all."

"What I'm not 'nice', grrr, I'm …I'm." I was trying to find the correct term.

"Full of yourself?" Andy cut in with a giggle.

"NO!" I protested, "Well maybe a little. But have you seen this?" I sent her a mind pic of me without a shirt, flashing my smile.

"Yes Joe, I have seen it, and yes, it is pretty impressive. I think I might send that to Mishie now," she said now laughing.

"Don't you dare," I growled.

"When am I going to see her again?" I enquired.

"When you do," Andy said.

"Not an answer," I growled.

"Haven't you got horses to work?" Andy said still laughing.

Chapter 20

I couldn't get her out of my mind. If I was with my horses, I was thinking about her. When I was eating, when I was driving and especially when I was sleeping. I couldn't believe I was so addicted to someone after just one meeting. I was anxious to see her again. I didn't even know you could have feelings for someone that were this strong. It was like she was the only reason I breathed now. I could still feel the tingles that went through my fingertips when we touched fingers at our first parting. Her face was permanently etched into my mind. I had forgotten the face of every other girl I had ever seen. There was just Mishie.

It was a whole three weeks of torture before I saw her again.

Andy woke me at some ridicules a.m., hour.

"Joe we have a mission, and we are running a little late because we had a bit of a mishap on the way."

I sat up in bed, "Everyone ok?" I asked concerned.

"Yes," Andy replied. She sent me mind pics of Mishie in a blue and white dress, some kind of costume I guessed, with bright red heals. Then I saw her flying through the air, the wind caught in her dress, and it billowing out like a sail. Her being blown of course and into a tree. Luckily Andy glittered her landing so she didn't get hurt. Mishie was upside down in the tree, her skirt around her neck, and the ugliest pair of white long frilly short things I had ever seen on her legs, with her red shoes sticking out. I started to laugh, "That's funny," I choked to Andy.

Andy was almost doubling over with laughter, "You should have been here!" She exclaimed between fits of hysterics.

Just then a very sweet little voice in my head, "Uh huh, laugh it up."

"Sorry, but it's kind of hilarious," I broke out laughing again.

"And hi Mishie," I added

"Uh huh," was the only reply I got.

Andy started to explain the details of our rescue. Two kids about ten and twelve were being bullied online, by a particularly nasty troll. Not only was it bullying them but it was trying to gather their personal information so it could pay them a nasty visit and they weren't the trolls only victims, but they were the first in the line for this troll. It then planned to move on to others. Andy explained that online bullies were the hardest for us to track down, and the Highers had been working on this one for about three months. Finally, we had the leads to put a stop to it.

We arrived at the address and I made us a doorway into the house. The boys were both here as they were having a sleep over. They were on the floor in sleeping bags. Mishie and I sat beside one boy each.

I put my hand on the elder boy's shoulder. For a few minutes there was nothing, then I found why. He was totally taken with Mishie, and he couldn't focus on anything else. I could hear his thoughts, he thought she was beautiful. I had to cut into his mind, uh, I searched for his name, Michael it was. "Um Michael," I said gently to him. He snapped back to reality. I winked at him and said, "Yeah she is!"

He grinned blushing scarlet red.

I whispered the magic words to him, **'Splendor et coruscent facit magicae'** at the same time Mishie did to his friend, both boys fell into their sleeping bags fast asleep.

We left the house.

On our way back home Mishie mind spoke to me, "Joe do you ever chase up on what happens to the bullies, after we complete our rescues?"

I replied, "No not usually. That's not my department."

"So, you're not interested in seeing what punishment they get?" she enquired.

"Nope, they get whatever they get. I have definite ideas on fitting punishments for crimes committed, but I guarantee the Highers don't share my ideas, so to save myself anger and disappointment I don't bother chasing it up," I responded.

"Ok," was the only answer she gave me, then she was silent for the rest of the trip. When we split to go our separate ways, I hovered for a bit in the sky watching them disappear. I knew deep down, she was going to be mine, one day, I just wish it would hurry up.

Now that Mishie had learned to mind-speak, she interrupted my mind throughout the day to ask me questions. It was great. I loved the sweet sound of her voice, tinkering inside my head.

She asked me about my wand, she asked about Andy's wand, she asked how many rescues I had been on? She asked about other G M F's? She asked if I had ever met an Osine? She asked if I'd ever met any Highers? She asked what I did for work?
Endless questions on and on.

I laughed at her, "Mishie, I will tell you all you need to know, in time ok?" There's no hurry though and we don't want to over load that sweet little brain of yours with too much information too quickly."

She mind sent me a pic of her sticking her tongue out at me. I sent her back one of my heart-breaker smile.

"And?" she said.

"Oh I'm crushed," I replied.

She giggled.

"Sigh" .....

"I can't tell you about Andy's stick as it isn't my place, but mine belonged to my deceased brother," I told her.

"I'm so sorry," she replied, somehow, she sent me a hug, like she was actually here.

"Ok, that's pretty weird, in a good way, but you, kinda, may wanna move now," I said... trying to override my body's basic desires.

"Or maybe not," she winked at me.

"Enough lessons for today," I growled.

I heard her still giggling, and I heard Andy's laugh as well, as I closed my mind off.

But I had a smile on my face for the rest of the day.

After Harry took the carrot from my hand, he and I had started to build our relationship back up. Now when I sat in the paddock, he would come up to me looking for treats. I was still going very slowly with him but I was able to touch his muzzle now. Sometimes, I would let Molly into the pen as well and she would come and sit with me and rest her head on my shoulders. I think this helped Harry too. He could see how much his mother loved me, and that she wasn't scared at all. I would love to know what had been done to him to make him so scared, but Andy had forbidden me from checking his mind.

She already knew, so I didn't need to scare the big stallion anymore. It was for my own good as I was still learning to control my temper. I was making great progress. I didn't need something to trigger it and send me backwards. It was better left unknown for now she had said. When the time was right, she promised to tell me. For now that was enough for me.

I had been slowly introducing shows back into Molly's routine. At first, we just watched. I kept her at a distance, so she couldn't be spooked. Then slowly we had been doing more. I bare-backed her around the ring and let her stop and sniff, and basically just go at her own pace. Two weeks ago I miss-timed, and took her out when the entertainment was just coming into the arena. There was a guy in the ring cracking a whip. My heart dropped to my toes, and my legs instinctively grabbed her sides tightly. Molly didn't miss a beat. I was so tense waiting for her to rare or bolt. She turned her head to look at me, as if to say what's your problem. I relaxed a little. She still wouldn't go to close though. Once we walked past another horse who had a ribbon on its neck, Molly tried to steal the ribbon. Ok ok I laughed, it is time for you to start winning your own again.

A few days later, I received an urgent message from Andy telling me to meet her at Mishie's place. I didn't have a clue where Mishie lived, luckily Andy did and she threw a map into my mind. Andy quickly explained, Mishie's sister had been in a bit of trouble and was currently missing, she said she would explain more later, but now I needed to be with Mishie. I glittered myself invisible, at Andy's instructions, and flew to Mishie's place. I could feel her sadness from kilometres away. I just needed to be there NOW, to hold her. My heart was breaking for her. When I landed in her yard, I walked behind a tree and glittered myself visible again. I walked into her parents' home like I owned the place, it wasn't intentional, I just didn't want to be standing around waiting for the door to be answered.

The hardest thing I have ever had to do, was let her go chasing her missing sister, Carly, alone, well not alone, she was going with Andy, but I wasn't going with her. I couldn't, I had responsibilities, here at the farm and to my horses but I was going to speak to dad, and see if I couldn't get a couple days away at the end of the week, if they were not back by then.

I threw myself into my work and the farm and spent every waking minute with my horses. I wasn't sleeping at all, so I had a lot of waking time, to try and take my mind off whatever Mishie was going through. I had very little communication since they had left, just Andy checking in once a day, telling me so far they had found nothing, but they were ok, although Mishie was getting sadder by the day.

While they were away, a couple of small rescues came up, that Rosemary, sent me to sort out on my own. She said I was more than capable of doing it, and that I did not need to hold Andy's hand all the time. I was shocked, as Rosemary and I weren't exactly best buddies. But I gladly accepted, not that I had any choice. It was more of a 'you will do this' and less of a 'could you please do this' situation. The first one was easy enough, a little girl being bullied by an old man and his dog in the park every day. The dog wanted to make friends with the little girl, who desperately needed a friend, and the stingy old cranky man, who kept yelling at her to get away from him and the dog. A couple times the dog had got away from the old man and run straight up to the little girl, licking her and wagging its tail. The old man came over and grabbed the dogs lead again and pulled it away, threatening the little girl that he would hit her with his cane if she did it again. It turned out the dog used to belong to the old guy's wife, who died a few months before, and he was overly protective of the dog now. When it was all dealt with, me dealing with the little girl, who was having nightmares of the old man hitting her with his walking stick, and the Highers dealing with the old man, the girl the old man and the dog all became good friends.

Rosemary esp'd me after it was said and done, "See Joe sometimes you just have to look a little deeper. What were your first instincts after seeing how the old man was being with the little girl?"

"I wanted to hit him with his cane," I said sheepishly.

"Exactly, but you see now why that would have been a mistake?" she responded.

"Yeah, I guess," I shrugged.

The second rescue wasn't quite so simple, and it left me feeling emotionally drained, and stirred up feelings I thought I had buried. Fifteen and fourteen-year-old sisters were being bribed and blackmailed by their mother, who was having an affair. The girls accidently walked in and saw their mother with another woman. The mother had seen them, and was now trying to stop them from telling their father. She was threatening them with all sorts of nastiness, including separating them, and changing their schools. Both girls were thought of highly in their high school and the fifteen-year-old was on track for an Olympic career in track and field, and possibly swimming. The fourteen-year-old was an academic, and had won awards in science and maths. She was set to receive a scholarship to one of the top colleges overseas. A change of schools would be devastating for them. The mother even told them she was going to tell their father they had been wagging school, and messing round with boys. A few days after I completed the rescue, Rosemary told me the mother had a job demotion, and ended up having to change continents, the girls' lives were going back to normal. Over time the long distance would take its toll, and the mother and father would separate of their own accord.

"You know I don't really care what happens to the bully," I told Rosemary, "They will never get their true punishments, your kind are way to forgiving. So, I really don't need you letting me know, it just makes me mad. I get the old guy and the little girl, both of them are way happier now than they were, the dog too. But when it comes to parents bullying their own kids, there will never be a punishment good enough for that!"

She sighed, "Probably best if we just don't talk about consequences for actions then."

Almost a week after they left, Andy sent me an ESP saying they had found Mishie's sister, but she wasn't in great shape. Andy wasn't sure if Carly would even make the next twenty-four hours. All going well they would be home soonish she hoped. There had been some drama with the guy who kidnapped her, and Rosemary had to step in. I stopped listening, Rosemary wasn't my favourite person but I sure would be glad to see Mishie again!

Chapter 21

After everything with Carly had settled down, and Mishie was permanently back in this state, during one of the many mind conversations we had, I asked her if she wanted to come to a horse show with me.

"Took you long enough," she said smiling.

We arranged to meet at the show grounds, as she did not want to be up at three a.m., on any weekend we weren't doing rescues. three a.m. was usually when she was just getting to bed sometimes even later, depending on where her latest gig was. I wasn't impressed with the three a.m. starts either, but grooming a horse until it's gleaming takes a lot of work, even with a horse as naturally stunning as Molly is.

She arrived in time to see Molly win her blue first ribbon of the day. Won in a relatively new show event, called the Lunge line. It was where each competitor had to attach lunge gear, harness and leads and lunge their horses in front of judges. The judges awarded points on the skill of the handler and of the horse. I had years of practise at lunging horses, and Molly had years of being lunged.

Mishie walked up to us, Molly was doing her 'look at me prance', showing off her ribbon. She made Mishie laugh.

"Show off," Mishie told her. This just made her head swell more. She was now reaching to her neck and trying to pull the ribbon off, so she could rub it in Mishie's face.

"She is so beautiful," Mishie said to me about Molly. "Can I pat her?" she asked.

"Absolutely, actually I can do one better than that," I winked at her.

I grabbed Molly's mane and swung myself up on her back then I reached down and grabbed Mishie's hand and swung her up behind me.

Mishie squealed, "I've never ridden before."

"I can tell, don't worry we will go slow, just relax," I told her.

She was squashing my insides she was holding so tight. No way was I complaining though.

We walked around the outside of the ring away from all the others. I commanded Molly to halt.

"Sit perfectly still," I told Mishie. I carefully stood up on molly's back, stepped over Mishie, and then sat down behind her. "Move forward," I whispered in her ear.

"What, what are you doing? I can't ride," she said trembling.

"It's ok I promise I told her, I'm right here, I won't let anything bad happen to you. Just relax ok."

Molly softly neighed as if agreeing with me.

We sat in the one spot for a few minutes. I was giving Mishie time to feel Molly. When Mishie was sitting a little better, and she was a bit more relaxed, I told her to gently squeeze her legs and rub her heels against Molly's side and say "Walk on."

Molly instantly started to walk. I had my arms around Mishie holding on to the lead rope. This way Mishie couldn't fall. Even if Molly shied at something, Mishie would be secure against me. It was pure torture. We walked back to Molly's float. I slid off, and helped Mishie down, she was grinning from ear to ear.

"That was amazing," and she hugged me.

I sighed into her. Mishie honey you're driving me nuts, I said to myself.

Luckily for me my barrel race was coming up and I needed to concentrate on something else for a while. I brushed Molly down and let Mishie help. Then I saddled her up and put myself on the back of Molly and pulled Mishie into the saddle. Her legs made it to half way down the stirrup leathers.

I pushed her knees into the saddle and told her to "Hold tension here." I reached around the front of Mishie and took up the reins. I squeezed Molly's sides gently with my thighs, and told her to "Canter up," Molly moved into a slow rhythmic canter.

"Got to warm her up." I said to Mishie in mind-speak.

Molly snorted, as if to say liar. Mishie was bouncing around in the saddle everywhere so I let go of the reins so I could reposition Mishie better in the saddle. Molly didn't miss a beat and just kept up her slow steady canter. I pushed Mishie's knees back against the saddle again and whispered into her ear, "You need to hold your knees firmly against the saddle and keep your calves in contact with the leather at all times. That's what's going to help you keep your balance. It will also stop you bouncing around. Hold pressure firmly with your thighs," I said to her. I put my arm around her waist and gently rocked her back and forth so as she matched my movements. We moved as one with the rhythm of the canter. She stopped trying to fight it and relaxed into my chest.

"You have to go with the movements. It's like a big ole rocking chair," I told her faking an American southern accent.

We reached the arena where my race was. I dismounted, then slid Mishie out of the saddle. I stood her aways away, over where the crowd had gathered, far enough so if a horse bolted, she wouldn't be in any danger.

"Wish me luck," I said to her. As I re-mounted Molly and rode off to wait my turn.

"Do you need it?" she asked as I rode away.

"Can never hurt," I replied in mind-speak.

"Uh huh, luck then," she said with a grin.

I was making Molly turn circles, stretching her legs where I could, keeping her warm. Barrels were a standing start, so she had to go from zero to top speed instantly, and I did not want her pulling a muscle or worse.

She stood in line to accept her blue ribbon patiently. Then she pranced away towards Mishie, all by herself. "You really are a show off," I said to her.

She neighed in agreement.

By the end of the day, Mishie was at least able to keep her balance on top of the mare, without me holding her. "I'll make a rider out of you yet," I said to her laughing.

We spent the day, in between mine and Molly's events, talking about G M F's. Mishie still in awe of her new found magic, had never ending questions, some I was able to answer, some not. I asked her lots of questions too. I found out she was in the most raved about band in Queensland. She told me how Andy had glittered a hologram-like figure of her while she was away looking for Carly. The band was in so much demand and she didn't want to let them down by not showing up for the booked in gigs. She also told me she was seriously thinking of giving it up to focus on composing instead. She said she wanted to spend more time at home. Some questions she evaded, anything about her family, or any details about what happened to Carly, she wouldn't answer. I guess we hadn't really known each other that long and she wasn't sure she could trust me.

What she didn't know was, I would give my life for hers in a heartbeat. I was an open book, anything she asked about myself, I answered truthfully. Ok I may have left a few little details out, like, um, you know my mother. Not because I didn't trust her with the shattered little pieces of my heart, but because I felt too ashamed of my mother to let anyone know what she had done. I told her as much about Kevin as I was able. I told her that before he died, he told me I would meet her, well not exactly her, but yeah. I also told her, that he said somewhere along the line, there would be another. We talked about Rex and Amelia, although I didn't really know them, and they were much older than I was, and we didn't really have a bond.

Right at the end of the day, after I had received my, 'Best of award', and Molly's 'Best of trophies' for the day, just as Mishie and I were packing Molly's saddles bridles and paraphernalia into the ute, out of the blue my last ex-girlfriend Lana, came walking up to us. You know sometime you just know the universe has just done a back flip, and the world is about to spin off its axis? Well, that's how I felt when I saw her, I knew trouble was coming my way.

"Hi, Joe," she said all fake-friendly-like. I groaned. I said hi back and introduced her to Mishie, except apparently, I said it wrong. Lana walked up and started to rub Molly down.

Molly started stomping her feet, and wasn't impressed at Lana touching her. It wasn't that she didn't like Lana, because she did, just not right now I guess. I said, "I didn't see you competing today?"

She said, "She hadn't, as my gelding pulled up lame. It is only just a temporary thing but he needs a few weeks rest."

We talked for a while about treatments and I said "I will call in to your place in a couple of days, and see if I could do anything to help her horse."

We talked for about an hour then she left. I turned to talk to Mishie, but she was gone. I finished packing up and searched around for Mishie, but she had left. I couldn't even get her to reply via mind-speak. Apparently, I had done something wrong! I finished loading Molly and headed home.

The whole hour and a half's drive home, I went over and over the unexpected meeting with Lana, but couldn't for the life of me figure out what I had done wrong. I pleaded in mind-speak with Mishie to talk to me, and tell me what I did wrong. There was just silence!

That night Andy called me for a mission. I joined her and Mish, hovering above my house.

"Hi," I greeted both of them cheerfully.

Mishie completely ignored me.

Andy speaking in my head, "What did you do Joe?" "I have no idea." I went over what had happened today to Andy in my head.

Andy asked me, "Joe in the short time you have known Mishie, what does she mean to you?"

I did not even have to think about it, the answer was automatic, "The world."

"And yet, you treated her like she was nonexistent", Andy replied.

"What? No, I didn't," I replied confused.

"Joe, you ignored her for over an hour, while your ex-girlfriend was purposely trying to distract, and flirt with you."

"NO and No, she wasn't, and I.... Mishie and I have a connection. I didn't think I needed to explain and it was all about the horse. I get carried away when I am discussing horses. Mishie is going to be, no, she is the **ONE**. I thought she knew that?" I attempted to explain.

"Have you told her?" Andy asked.

"I thought she could feel what I was feeling, you know a two-way G M F matched for life thing. I what I was, I didn't think I needed to spell it out, or shout it from the roof tops, I would have done that if I had of known," I said.

"Joe," was all Andy added.

We were flying over the botanical gardens, not overly high up and I could see some rose bushes in flower below.

"Be right back," I said to Andy.

I flew down to where I thought the roses were, except I wasn't really concentrating. I was hurting because I had without knowing, hurt the only girl I ever wanted to see for the rest of my life. With all the reflective lights, that were used to light up the trees in all different colours, I misjudged, and ended up flying, straight through a very shallow pond. The pond was full of mud and water Lilies and sleeping ducks, except they weren't exactly sleeping now. Now they were screaming murder, and waking the whole city up and trying to catch me and bite me. As I was trying to fly out, I got my foot tangled in a water Lily and ended up landing face first in mud mixed with years of duck poo. I managed to crawl out of the pond, covered in mud and duck-weed, and dragging a tangled water Lily with me, only then to stand in a nest of rotten duck eggs right at the edge of the pond.

Mishie and Andy had flown down to see if I was ok, and were standing safely on the grass, about five metres away from the pond right in the middle of the roses, I was looking for. Mishie was rolling around on the grass by the time I walked up to them, she wasn't even able to talk. Every time she looked at me, all she could say was "OMG," and burst out laughing again. Andy was faring a little better, "What were you doing?" she asked between fits of hysterics.

"The plan was to pick Mishie some roses," I said sheepishly.

One of them, flashed a picture into my mind of what I looked like. I looked like a weird alien/swamp/jungle creature. I had weed stuff hanging from my head, I was covered in mud and duck poo and had bits of bright green duck-weed stuck to me everywhere. I had water Lily pads and roots trailing behind me, and tangled around my legs. I didn't need anyone to send me the smell. I could smell, rotten egg, rotten mud, and duck poo, and it covered me. Andy recovered enough to wave her stick over me, and send glitter cascading over my head and within seconds I was clean, fresh and smelt like new again. I went to where Mishie was now sitting on the grass, holding her sides, and offered her my hand to help her up. To my surprise she took it. I walked over to the nearest rose bush, it was a dusty pink coloured rose, I snapped it off, and handed it to her.

"I'm sorry" I said, "Can you please give me a chance to explain?"

She took the rose and said, "Yes, but not now ok?"

I had to be ok with that.

We all flew off to finish the mission.

Chapter 22

This mission was a little different to the others, and I wasn't sure why we were here, it's not something we usually get involved in, but I guess Andy had her reasons. We stopped at fairly modern brick house with a big yard. It had a cubby house complete with a slide and sandpit, swing set, and a pool. The house itself was pretty big. I magic'd us up a doorway, that led us right into a kid's bedroom. But instead of being awake and sitting on the bed waiting for us, the little boy was sound asleep. I shot a 'what the hell' look at Andy, she shrugged, and answered in my mind, "I don't know."

We quietly made our way to another bedroom, but it was the same, the little girl was sound asleep. We left the way we had came. When we were airborne again, I said, "Well that was pretty strange, you sure you had the right address Andy?"

"Definitely, and yes that was strange. In all my years I have never came across that," Andy answered.

"So, what was the go there? Why were we there?" I enquired.

"Those two little ones, are being severely bullied by their elder sister and while sibling stuff isn't usually something we get involved in, this mission came straight from Rosemary," Andy said.

I could see Andy was preoccupied and guessed she was trying to contact Rosemary. Contacting the

Highers wasn't always easy, so I let her have some quiet to do it.

I reached out to Mishie via mind-speak, "Can I explain now?" I asked.

"No," she replied.

"Ok," I sighed, my heart dropping to my toes.

After a few minutes, Andy Esp'd us what Rosemary had said, apparently the older sister, had given the children a sleeping tablet. She somehow known we would be there tonight, although we have no Idea how. As we only get one chance per child, per bully, the children being asleep means the rescue could never go ahead. Which means the sister, whose name is Ashley, will now get away with whatever she is doing to her brother and sisters, and will go unpunished. So, she will be free to bully lots of others as well. Rosemary said it's a sad day for us fairies, as Ashley is going to pop up again in the future, and cause havoc, where as if we could have stopped her tonight, the future would look a lot brighter.

We all headed to our homes. I was exhausted, and as soon as I lay in my bed, I was immediately asleep.

I was awoken by someone banging on my door and I stumbled out to open the door, in my pj bottoms. When I opened the door the sun was shining brightly. I had to blink a few times for my eyes to adjust. Standing on my door step was Mishie.

I wanted to wrap her up in my arms and never let her go. Just the sight of her made my heart skip a beat. "Um hi," she said looking at my half naked body and blushing.

"Morning," I said.

"Except it's after lunch time," she replied.

"What! Are you kidding?" I said in disbelief.

"Mish I really want to talk to you, and if you come to the kitchen and make yourself at home for an hour or so while I rush around and do my chores, I promise I will then give you the rest of the day," I pleaded.

She reluctantly agreed.

I flew into the shower, and got dressed, then ran out to the stables, gave Molly a kiss on the muzzle on my way past, promising I would be here later to talk to her. I completed my chores in record time. Harry was watching me from his paddock softly neighing at me, I took the time to walk to his gate, hoping he would come to the gate to get a pat. He stood just out of arms reach. I sighed and raced back to the house.

I came back in to see her sitting at the breakfast bar talking to my grandma and aunt, drinking coffee and eating croissants. I sat beside her and had coffee as well.

Mishie didn't look like she was in a hurry.

I said to her in mind-speak, "After we finish our coffee, would she be ready to go and talk."

She told my aunt and grandma it was nice to meet them, then we walked out to the fire pit area.

"Well start explaining Joe, because at the moment I am mad as hell with you," Mishie said.

"I'm sorry, I.. well ... I ... um... grrr. I, I thought we were on the same page Mish. I never imagined you would get jealous of someone who would never and has never meant as much to me as you do. I thought you felt the same as I do. The first time I met you I knew you were the one, the only one. Ever! No one has ever even come close. I'm not trying to brag here, but there has been a lot of girls Mishie, and with every single one of them it never felt right. I was never fully relaxed with them. They never quite 'fit' me. You do Mish. You and me we 'fit'. It's not hard, I don't have to work at it, it just is. I have never felt this way about anyone. You're the belt to my jeans, you complete me, like nothing and no one ever has before. I want you beside me for the rest of time. You never have to worry about any other girl/woman, living or dead ever. I can't ... Don't know how else to put it .... I'm yours Mish, nothing you could ever do or say will change that. Do you understand what I am saying to you... Please Mish, don't push me away. I can't breathe without you." ....I poured my heart out to her, I didn't tell her I loved her, I did, but I didn't want to scare her away. I loved her the first minute I looked into those huge lilac eyes. Actually, truth be told I have loved her forever, but I have only just found her.

I dared a glance at her, she was sitting perfectly still. No emotion on her face at all. A single lonely tear running down her cheek.

Damn I had made her cry, I felt like a real ass now.

I was beside her in an instant and grabbed her hand and held it. "Mishie I'm sorry whatever I said that made you cry, I'm sorry and I take it back."

"Don't you dare take it back, I have never in my life heard such heart felt words, I didn't just hear what you were saying Joe, I felt it here." She took my hand and placed it over her heart.

She stood up, and threw her arms around me. I put my arms around her too. She really did fit me, like she was made for me. Neither of us had to duck or bend to shape our bodies, we were a perfect fit, for each other.

"Joe, I feel the same, that's why I got upset. I thought I must have been the only one feeling it, and I was angrier at myself for jumping in feet first, without testing the depth of the water. I wasn't jealous of her Joe, I was upset because you forgot I was there," She stated.

"Mish as long as I live, this life and everyone after, I will never forget you're there. This I promise you," I told her.

She pulled her head back slightly and looked up at me, her eyes and mine locked, our souls connecting and becoming one now and forever.

Then she kissed me, like I had never been kissed before.

Forget the fireworks, the whole freaking world exploded around me, I think there was an eightpoint million earth quake right under the spot we were standing. She sighed in my mind, the sigh of complete and total bliss. I never wanted this moment to end. If I died right now from lack of oxygen, then I'd die with a smile on my face.

Chapter 23

Now that we were officially a couple, life became a lot easier. We knew what each other was thinking, even without mind-speak. I ended up telling her about what my mother had done, and about how I reacted and beat the guy with the whip. By the time I finished telling her the story, I was crying again. It's not something I am proud of, and I doubt I will ever be able to think about it without feeling horrible and ashamed and ... like a total head case. Mish didn't accuse me, or get angry with me, she just held me, and let me cry. She didn't even tell me it was ok, she just held me. I was glad she didn't try to make excuses for me, I didn't deserve them, I had been in the wrong, and that was something I had to live with. I told her what I had done, after visiting the hospital and those little kids. I explained that I knew it didn't make up for my actions in the first place. She smiled and commented she was glad I did. I also let her know I hadn't told anyone else what I had done and I really didn't want Andy or Rosemary to know. Andy interrupted my mind and said they already knew. I may have blocked her and Rosemary from my mind that night but because of everything that happened earlier that day, the other Highers were watching me. None of the Highers were convinced that Rosemary had done the right thing by giving me another chance. But after that act of complete selflessness, I had won all them all over.

Chapter 24

One rainy stormy night a few days after mine and Mishie's heart to heart, Andy called us for a meeting in the park. Mishie and I were early so we sat huddled on a picnic table, covered by a tin roof, with lightening lighting the night sky every few seconds, and the thunder cracking loud enough to shake the ground. We waited for Andy and she eventually mind-spoke to us an hour after we turned up. She explained there had been a change of plans, and could we meet her in the burger place further down the road. She told us that we would have to walk as it was too dangerous to fly in this storm. By the time we got to the meeting place Mish and I were soaked through. We glittered ourselves dry and headed inside. Both Andy and Rosemary were waiting at the table.

"This should be fun," I whispered to Mishie, she elbowed my ribs and told me to behave and then linked her arm around my back and snuggled herself into me. We sat together on the opposite side of Andy and Rosemary.

Andy got up and went to the counter to order us all some food and coffee.

Rosemary looked really upset. She announced that here had been an attack by an Osine on a Glitter Magic Fairy in America yesterday. The Fairy didn't make it, he was tortured and then killed. He hadn't been a fairy long, and the Osine made short work of him. Thank-fully he never gave permission for the glitter the Osine had gathered to be used.

In the last twenty-four hours there had been another seven attacks, with two of the fairies still being held prisoner by Osine, and another in a critical condition in a hospital bed in England. Rosemary continued on to say they didn't know what was going on. They were unprepared because there hadn't been Osine uprising for a long long time. Andy came back with our food, we all started to eat in silence. Andy interrupted the silence saying, "The whole Glitter Fairy Organisation was on high alert, and were urging all Fairies to be on their guard."

She was about to say more when Rosemary interrupted her, "There's been an attack in Perth, the G M F is very shaken, but thankfully unhurt. It was a fully trained GM F that had been a fairy for about 10 years."

Andy looked worried, "You two need to be super careful," she told us, "No taking any silly chances. We will only go on rescues together the three of us. No waiting around outside the rescue's homes, we all go in together. This is very bad."

Rosemary stood up, "I have to go," she rushed. "I will keep you as updated as I can," she said into our minds as she was leaving. "PLEASE be careful guys. No one in our family wants to see any more Fairies hurt, taken or killed."

Andy sighed, "Its bad, very bad. You both know all I can tell you about the Osine. I have just received notification that a new fairy will be joining us soon. With the Osine attacks we can expect an influx of new Fairies. Trouble is, they will all need training, and I won't be able to watch you two as much as I would like to, which means sometimes you will **have** to be on your own. I HATE the thought of it." She had tears in her eyes, "Please promise me you will look after and protect each other."

I gave her my most charming smile, "That is something you can be one hundred percent sure of. I will never let anything happen to Mish," I said truthfully.

Three nights after our meeting, Andy called Mishie and I to go to a rescue of sorts, a group of about ten, twelve and thirteen- year-olds had formed themselves a small gang. Andy said that they were mostly good kids, but were bored and had nothing else to do. They had taken to sneaking out of their houses at night, after their parents were sleeping and terrorizing the streets of Surfers. There were a couple of harmless old guys living behind the surf shed. They didn't have much, but managed to get by. One of them did some busking outside the local shops while the other one would walk to the marina every day, hoping to get some work with the trawlers, bringing in their daily catches. At the very least, because he was well known at the marina, a couple of the trawler captains would give him a couple of fresh fish and a ½ a bucket of prawns to take home. The gang had stolen the busker's guitar and smashed it to pieces. They had also terrorized a few tourists that headed down for a midnight swim, stealing their clothes and wallets. Or worse their car keys, then taking the car for a joy ride through the streets. None of them knew how to drive and so they were a danger to everyone.

Andy said we had to deal with them now before they ruined their lives, and some innocent person's life for ever.

Andy gave us the address of their meeting place and Mishie and I headed there after eleven pm and waited for them to show up. It was a small concrete pad, that was sealed on three sides by tall colour-bond fencing panels. The fourth side had a timber arbour built into it and there was a door way into the area, which had two half sized unlocked timber gates. There was a street light at the front of the area across a main road which ment only the front of the place was lit up.

I hadn't done a reverse rescue before, neither had Mishie, so we were following Andy's strict advice. At about 11.15pm the kids started to file into the area. Mishie and I were hidden in a dark shadowed corner and we had glittered ourselves so as we couldn't be seen yet. Andy was watching the group via my mind. When they were all there, she gave us the signal to start the rescue. Mishie and I put up a temporary barrier over the exit, so the gang couldn't get away. We exited our hiding place and glittered ourselves visible again. The kids all panicked at seeing us there and tried to scramble out the door. We sternly told them all to sit on the ground in a circle, or they would be locked in here and the local authorities would be called. By some miracle they did what we asked. When they were all seated, Mishie took one side and I took the other. We made them put their fingertips on the shoulder of the person beside them, this way we were able to clearly communicate will all of them at once. We ESP'D them the images of what they had done to people, they thought it was funny. Then we showed them images of what was going to happen to them if they continued down this path. They were not laughing anymore. Most started crying and wanted to go home, but of course there were always the ones that couldn't be told, and Mishie and I knew they were going to be ones we would have to take care of when they were older. After promises were made by most of them to pull their heads in and stop this current behaviour, we released the barriers and let them go. We tracked all of them in our mind. Eight went straight home and the other two went and broke bottles at a public toilet block. We were going to deal with them but Andy said via ESP "To leave it. Their time and punishment would come."

The next day I visited a music store and brought a brand-new guitar. I had it wrapped with a big red bow and later that night I walked behind the surf shed and left it where the old busker would find it. I added a note to say how sorry I was. I knew he would think it was from the kids that broke it, and that was ok with me.

Mishie ESP'd me "Why did you do that?"

I told her the guitar was the old guy's dignity, he wasn't begging for handout, he was earning an honest living, and without the guitar, he would feel as though all his hope was gone. I wanted to give him back that hope, and maybe a little bit of spark that humanity was still alive.

In the next few months, the Osine attacks were getting more daring. Andy was stuck with the new recruit, apparently, he had a lot to work through, and he wasn't making much progress. Typical of Andy though, she wasn't very forthcoming with information. I had been sent to do a few more simple rescues on my own, some I was supposed to take Mishie with me, but there were some things going on with her work at the moment that she had to sort out. I am trying to give her space and time to do it. The things with work had been distracting her for a couple of months and she really needed to get them under control so she could stay focused on the rescues and not get herself hurt.

I have been spending as much time as I could with Harry. It seemed as though I take one step in the right direction one week, and the next, he'd revert back to being scared. I am getting very close to having to use glitter on him. I don't want to, and it's not that I have anything against the glitter but I just really wanted him to come round on his own. Andy has said she thinks maybe it's time I found out what happened to him. I wanted to know what happened to him but I was scared of what it might do to me, if I knew. But at the same time, if I knew, I guess I could work with it, instead of just trying to guess what going on in that brain of his. At least I would know why he has been reacting the way he has been.

Molly has been trying to help. If I am working with him, I let her into his pen. She seems to have a calming influence on him. I have to be a little bit careful with her at the moment as she is in foal. I don't know who the father is, as it happened the night they were let out so it could be anyone of six stallions. Or it could be a stallion I don't know as I have no idea where they were kept or what they were paddocked with when they were taken.

A few weeks later, I decided I would finally try and find out what had happened to Harry that night. I'd had a particularly bad work session with him that day, where he just seemed to totally forget who I was. His eyes rolled back in his head, and he seemed to see me as the enemy. He actually charged me, tried to corner me, and reared up trying to strike me with his hooves. I sat outside the door on his stable, in the quiet of night. He wouldn't appreciate me being in there with him, and if he got spooked, in that tight space, he may have actually seriously hurt himself or me. Usually he was opposite Molly, but this night I put him beside her because I thought it might help to calm him down. I had put a mild sedative in his food, that vet prescribed it for him. It was for when he was really agitated, and I had only used it twice in the time that I'd had the horses back. I waited until he had settled down for the night, and the sedative was starting to take effect, then I snuck into his stall. I had a small vial of Rosemaries glitter, which she normally wouldn't give out. It would be too dangerous if it fell into the wrong hands. With all the attacks lately, I practically had to sign my soul over to her, before she would give it to me. I blew the glitter on his muzzle, then I contacted Andy and said I was ready. Even with Rosemary's glitter I still wasn't able to look far enough into his mind to where he had the trauma situated on my own. Andy was going to do it and relay it straight into my mind. She already knew most of what happened to him as Rosemary had told her. I have to admit I was apprehensive of what I would find. I wished I had Mishie here to lean on if I needed her, but she was doing band stuff, and I hadn't told her what I was doing.

Chapter 25

It was worse than I could have ever imagined and my heart sunk. No wonder I was getting nowhere. The guy had entered the stables in the early hours of the morning and he opened the stalls and let all the other horses out of the stables. Before he entered the stable, he must have opened all the paddock gates. He had also been through dads stable and let all his horses into the paddocks. That's why, when I found them the next morning, they were all mixed up. I'm not sure why he did that though. He knew which horse Harry was and he's a big horse and he stands out. The guy wasn't sure which horse Molly was and he'd accidently let her out. He tried to get her before she left the stable, but because he had panicked the horses, they were all running together and he couldn't catch her. Because Harry sensed something was wrong, he started rearing and pounding the dirt in his stable. He was kicking out at the walls, and charging at the gate trying to get out to save his mares. He was calling out to them and the more he couldn't get out to them, the more agitated he became. The guy had now left the stables and was still trying to track Molly down, that's when he brought out his whip. The horses had all combined and there were stallions mixed in with mares. The stallions took exception to him being anywhere near the mares, and tried to kill him. Molly had distanced herself from the rest of the herd. Her foal was to dad's big buckskin stallion. That's how he managed to catch her. He had thrown a rope around her neck and hid behind a fence post, off to the side until the stallion had moved away. But she fought him, and tried to shie away, biting at him, and kicking out. He managed to get her to the float he had parked near the stables, but no way was she going in. That's when she received the whippings.

All this time Harry was still going crazy in the stables, he had all but managed to kick his stable door down. When the guy finally had Molly loaded and he got back to the stables, Harry was wild and totally skitzing out. The guy knew at any second Harry was going to break through the stall. He run back to his car, and grabbed an injection out of it. He went back into the stables, and injected it into Harry's neck. I don't know what it was, but it wasn't meant for horses. It caused him to have a violent reaction. I would never have imagined the horror that my poor horse went through that night. Because I was his trainer, and the only human who ever worked him and because of the drugs that were injected into him he blamed me. He seen me doing all those things to him, and not the actual guy that had. He was beaten, he was hit with a high-powered cattle prod, he had his feet bound front to back causing him to fall and damage and bruise his side. He had dogs set upon him and he was put into the same paddock as another stallion, although only a pony. The guy that had taken him, tried to ride him, but he threw him off, that is what earned him the cattle prod. Every time the guy went near him, he flicked his whip across his back, or punched his muzzle. By the time the glitter had worn off, and the images were starting to fade I was a mess. The fact that he blamed me, that he thought I could ever do something like that to him, was my end. I had no words. It was like it had all just happened again. I left the stables, got in my 4x4, and just drove. I couldn't face Harry ever again, even though I knew I hadn't done it, he thought I had. It was well after midnight and I drove for hours, not really knowing where I was heading, just needing to not be around anymore. I wouldn't cause my poor horse any more anguish. I was hardly concentrating on the road, lost in my own thoughts and I drove through a bad storm, the road slippery after being dry for so long. I lost control on a curve, the back end of the ute skidding on the wet road with me unprepared for it. The car rolled over and over, I lost count of how many times, down an embankment. It came to a stop embedded sideways in a huge old gum tree.

Chapter 26

I woke-up in a hospital bed, no idea how I got there, or how long I had been there. The curtains were all drawn so I didn't even know if it was day or night. I ached everywhere. As I began to focus my eyes I could make out a shape in a chair beside my bed. I tried to get myself in a sitting position. The figure in the chair, jumped up, pushed the button on the bed to make it lift to a sitting position. In the next instant I was being yelled at. "WHAT THE HELL DO YOU THINK YOU WERE DOING? YOU ARE ONE LUCKY S.O.B.! YOU SHOULD YOU BE DEAD! OMG SON WHAT THE HELL MADE YOU PULL A STUNT LIKE THAT?"

The next thing, big strong arms surrounded me, and I could feel him shaking. He pulled me back to look at me, he had tears falling down his face, and looked like he hadn't slept in a month.

"Dad," I managed to croak out, "What the hell happened? I remember, rolling down the hill, I remember the tree, but I don't remember anything from then on."

"Did you have an argument with Mishie? Is that what it was all about? Because if you were trying to kill yourself over some chick, then I failed as a parent," dad replied, without answering my question.

"What! No! Mishie and I are not arguing. You wouldn't understand dad, but Harry blames me for everything that happened to him that night," I stated.

Dad was shakings his head. "You couldn't possibly know that, son, you just think he does. He knows you. He loves you."

I couldn't explain it to him. How was I supposed to tell him, I had my friend read the horses mind, and that Harry one hundred percent blamed me. He would have me committed. In all honestly maybe he should.

Just then a doctor walked into my room and told me I was the luckiest person he knew. I had sustained no series injuries, just some lacerations, none that needing stitching, and bruising. I was ok to go home. He said, "I would be a little stiff and sore for a few days, and I had to watch out for signs of a head injury."

I thanked him.

I asked dad where my clothes were, as I was currently in a hospital gown. He threw a paper bag containing my belongings on the bed which had my jeans, shirt, watch, phone and wallet in it. The clothes were spotless with no traces they had even been worn. I pulled them out and noticed the glitter in the bottom of the paper bag.

Dad and I walked out to his 4x4, and drove home in silence. When we arrived at home, he locked the car doors, and turned to me and said, "Joe I don't know what's got into you. You say you're not arguing with your girlfriend. You tell me everything is ok, but then you pull a stunt like this."
I tried to interrupt but he shut me down.

"I don't want to hear any more about the horse blaming you. It's a damn horse, not a human. If you can't work out how to get around his problem, and I have to say after all this time, it's not looking like you will, then we may have to consider other options for him. You have responsibilities to the rest of your horses. You can't be singling out just one horse. How would I ever cope without you? You know I won't hire help, after what happened with the last lot of help we hired. Did you stop to think of your grandmother? Or anyone else? How would they cope if you died? They wouldn't get through it Joe. It would kill them as well. I have already lost one son to a car accident. I'm just so damned disappointed in you right now son."

He finished speaking. I had never seen him look so defeated.

"I wasn't trying to kill myself, I just needed to get away from everything. I wasn't paying attention to the road, it was wet, the back of the ute skidded out. I wasn't quick enough to correct it. I went over the embankment. I swear dad, it wasn't intentional.
I am sorry that you think so little of me, that you think I would intentionally try to harm myself. For the record Harry **won't** be going anywhere, I don't know how, but I will find a way to break through to him again.

I know I have responsibilities. More of them then you will EVER know about. I know a lot of people love me. I know I have to be here to run this stud, because mostly you're not that good at it. Lastly, and the only other reason I have for never purposely doing anything like suicide, is because of Kevin. I have to live my life for him. So, no dad I wasn't trying to harm myself..... Where is my car?" I finished, angry because he thought so little of me.

"What's left of your car is parked around the back of your stable, it's unfixable though. And maybe when you see it you will get an idea of just how close to being dead you came. I have already organised another one for you, it will be delivered this afternoon." With that, he unlocked the doors and removed himself from the car and strode off. Leaving me to struggle out of the car on my own.

I wasn't prepared to go inside the house yet, as I knew what was going to be waiting for me in there.

I headed to molly's paddock, she came up to me and nuzzled against me. I told her she was the only thing in the world that had ever understood me. I could see my big stallion a few paddocks away, watching me. I cried into Molly's mane. "I didn't do it Moll, why can't he see what really happened and who did hurt him?" I slid to the ground, my ever-faithful mare kneeling down beside me, then rolling onto her side and curling her body around me, tucking her legs in to hold me in place. As always, I felt warm and protected by Molly. I lay my head back on her belly and started at the blue sky, mesmerized watching the fluffy white clouds drifting by.

I must have fallen asleep, as I was startled awake by someone tapping my shoulder. When I opened my eyes, the sun was starting to go down and Mishie and Andy were both standing there.

I could see Mishie had been crying. Molly neighed softly and then awkwardly got up, she nuzzled Mishie, then trotted off to the far fence line to talk to another mare.

Andy reached out her hand to help me up. As soon as my feet were flat on the ground. Mishie flew into my arms almost knocking me back down. "Joe I was so worried about you," she wailed. "Don't you EVER do that to me again. I thought you were going to die." She held me tighter.

For a tiny little woman she sure had some grip. Andy joined in the hug, my bruises were all hurting, but no way was I going to tell them to move away. I put my head in Mishie's hair and it smelt like sunshine and coconut. I wrapped my arms around her and held her tighter. We broke away then I walked around to the back of my stables to see my car. Andy and Mishie followed me. I stopped as soon as I had a visual on the car. I gulped hard. It was worse than I thought. The whole driver's side had been crushed, and was now in the passenger's side. The bonnet was crushed to where the windshield should have been, there was now no windshield. The back of the car was relatively undamaged. I looked at Andy, and stated, "I should be dead."

She nodded. "Rosemary," was all she said.

"You do know I wasn't purposely out to hurt myself?" I uttered.

"If you were trying to consciously do something silly, I don't think Rosemary would have bothered helping you," Andy replied. "But you were angry Joe, and you did leave here in no state to be driving. So, I don't really know what you were thinking. But what I do know is, it's time we fixed that horse of yours. Yes, we will have to use Glitter. I should never have let it go this far, I was hoping Harry would see you weren't the bad guy on his own, but he was so drugged out and confused that night, that nothing you do will allow him to see the truth of it. So, it's time, I don't ever want to see you in the state we found you in, in that car ever again. It is past time we put those demons in your head to rest. Do you understand?"

"Did you bring me back to life?" I asked.

"Thankfully no, you were still alive when we got to you. You were slipping away and I didn't think we were going to be able to help you. Rosemary and a Higher, a Higher that's way higher than her, agreed to help you because of how you helped the guy that stole you horses and his kids. They worked on you for hours Joe, and had to revive you twice. Those light bruises you see now are nothing compared to what you did look like. I had to hide the accident scene and the trashed car from other motorist. If someone had of seen the wreck and called an ambulance, you wouldn't still be here."

I shuddered at the thought. "So, what do we do about Harry?" I asked as I started to walk away from the wreak. To be honest, I'd be happy to never see it again. I would have to go through it at some point though, as it had a pile of documents I needed in it.

"Nothing until you have had a chance to rest. Tomorrow you're going to be sore, real sore. Mishie and I are going to help you get your chores done, then we are going to set up camp in the clearing where the fire pit is, because we are not leaving your side for a few days. Rosemary will be visiting us later, she has some things she wants to say to you!" Andy stated.

I realised Mishie hadn't said much in the last fifteen or so minutes, she had just been hanging off my arm. I tried to reach her via mind-speak, but she had me blocked out. I stopped walking long enough to pull her away from me and look down at her. She had tears streaming down her face. "Oh baby," I muttered and I pulled her into my arms, her sobs causing her whole body to shake. "It's ok, I'm ok, I'm so sorry to have hurt you. I always seem to be hurting you, Baby, please don't cry." I reached down and scooped her into my arms and she curled into my chest and rested her head against it. I carried her one handed to the clearing about eight hundred metres away from where we currently were.

I knew at some point I was going to have to go inside and face my grandmother.

I really just did not want to. The disappointment in her eyes would be devastating, and although I know I didn't set out to have the accident, trying to convince her of that was going to be a task in its self.

It Turned out, I didn't need to. Andy had just finished glittering us a camp site, complete with tents, sleeping bags etc. The camping stuff had been stored in the shed, and not used since before mum, dad and Kevin's accident all those years ago. She just glittered it from there to here, and then used her glitter to set it all up. I had lit the fire drum from scratch as there hadn't been a fire in here for weeks. I saw my grandmother and Aunty both heading into our camp. I gave the others a heads up. I had a small chuckle to myself at trying to explain about glitter magic to them. I introduced them to Andy. They had already met Mishie.

"Well boyo you had better start explaining," my Grandma said, placing a large plate of lasagne, a bowl of tossed salad, plates and cutlery on the log table in the middle of the circle. aunt Denny had a cooler full of wine, soft drink and cans of assorted alcohol. "I didn't know what everyone liked to drink," she explained, "So I just brought some of everything."

Before I said anything I mind spoke Andy to make sure Rosemary didn't suddenly appear while my other family was here.

Grandma dished out the food, and passed it around.

It was the best tasting lasagne I had ever eaten. "It's not what you think," I told my grandma. I proceeded to explain some of what had happened and I told them about not making any headway with Harry, but left out that he blamed me for everything that happened to him. When I finished my story, I looked at my grandma and I could see she had believed what I told her, I breathed a sigh of relief. We finished eating, and grandma and aunt Denny started to pack up the dirty dishes to take back inside. Mishie got up to help, but they shoo'd her away, so she sat back down beside me. aunt Denny was about to pick the cooler of drinks up and take them back inside.

"They can stay," I winked at her. I was pretty sure I was going to need a couple more.

Rosemary flew into camp about an hour later. I started to explain to her, but she held up her hand to stop me. "I don't want your excuses, Joe. I know what you were thinking, I know you weren't concentrating on the road. You have had so many chances and warnings, you are just lucky my superior has taken a shine to you, or we wouldn't be having this conversation right now."

Mishie snuggled into me tighter, it felt like she was trying to crawl inside of me.

Rosemary continued, "There are no more chances for you Joe, pull your act together, or your out. Do you understand?"

She didn't give me a chance to reply.

"We are having enough issues at the moment with the Osine attacks, you're not the centre of our world. We cannot and will not be baby-sitting you twenty-four hours a day, from now on you are on your own Mr. While we were trying to save your life yesterday, three G M F's were caught overseas, and haven't been heard of since."

"I did **not** ask for you to step in and save me," I replied angrily. "I appreciate it, but don't go accusing me of taking up your time or trying to make me feel guilty because others got captured."

"Joe, do you have any idea what would have happened to Mishie or Andy, had you of died?" Rosemary said to me in mind-speak.

I shrugged. She flashed images of Mishie, walking the streets at night wearing only rags, her heart broken, and her feet dragging, her eyes empty no longer a fairy, not quiet a human anymore either. Andy leading some G M F's in war against the Osine, a war we lost. G M F bodies lying on the ground covered with white sheets. Other G M F's chained and being dragged along like dogs behind Elder Osine. One image showed Andy beaten and battered, left to die in a pool of her own blood. The images brought tears to my eyes. Your destiny is tied to another's, without the both of you together, we have no hope of winning the war that's coming. And this is the fate of your loved ones and friends if you don't start to step up and be the person you were meant to be.

Occasionally we see glimpses of that man, but Joe we need to see him all the time! The others can't see the images I just showed you. I will be erasing them from your mind, but leaving enough of the feeling left so you know it's up to you to bring your best game, or everything you care about will be lost forever. I have given Andy a little bit more of my glitter, so as you can try again to fix Harry. You get one chance Joe, if it doesn't work, find another use for him, and move on with your life."

With that she was gone.

Chapter 27

Andy wasn't kidding, the next morning my whole body ached, including the tips of my fingers. I couldn't even get out of my sleeping bag. I had to call both Mishie and Andy into my tent to help me sit up. The slightest movement of my body caused spasms of pain to radiate through my back and down my legs. Both Andy and Mishie concentrated their glitter on getting me up and moving. As they were helping me out of my tent, grandma showed up with muffins, bacon, eggs, fried tomato, and barbeque sauce, and a large jug of freshly squeezed orange juice. She looked at me and said, "A bit sore this morning are we?"

I growled in response, but was very thankful for the food.

It took three days for me to be able to walk without my body screaming in pain. Mishie my angel, the love of my life, never left my side. Andy however had to leave early the second morning before the sun was up, some crisis with the new fairy, "I swear you boys are out to kill me," she said with a wink before flying off.

Molly was helping Mishie with my chores, she even let Mishie ride her around the arena a couple of times, it was the only exercise she was going to get, there was no way I could even climb on her, let alone sit upright. I gave Mishie some simple instructions on how to lunge horses, and my father helped her put the lunge gear on, and showed her how it worked. I stood propped up on the fence while she had a go. I only let her do a couple of the quieter older mares, that were so used to it, they pretty much put themselves through their paces. I knew it would make Mishie feel like she was helping.

Pain aside, having Mishie so close to me for days at a time was the happiest I had been in a hell of a long time.

A week after I had all but become normal again, Andy called us to a mission. She told us via Esp that we would be meeting the new Glitter Magic Fairy tonight, and to take it easy on him, as he has had a really bad time of it lately. I flashed her an image of my wreaked 4x4. She said that only involved myself, he had family stuff going on. She never elaborated anymore than that.

We met them just south of the Queensland boarder, at a popular tourist spot. I had flown to Mishie's house then we had both flown to the spot, and had sat on the beach watching the waves crash in the moonlight, waiting for Andy and the new fairy. Andy introduced us to Alfie, he had bright red/orange hair, cut short at the back but long on the top, so it hung to his eyes. He wore a pair of square black rimmed glasses, which made his gold eyes look huge. It looked as though he had no pupil in his eyes, just a black fleck through the gold. But when you looked closely, he actually had an almost clear pupil, there was no colour to it at all, and you could see the blood vessels in his inner eye through it. He had a few freckles splattered around his cheeks, and he was bulkier and musclier than I was.

Although not quite as tall. He wore faded fitted stonewashed jeans and a grass green coloured shirt. His wings were magnificent, midnight black, shaped like massive bat wings, complete with the little sharp piece of bone-like claw in the middle. Mishie, wolf whistled, "Oh, very nice!" she exclaimed on seeing him. I pretended to sulk. But strangely enough I wasn't jealous or upset, he was very good looking, although he didn't have my charm. When the introductions were over, Andy told us the rescue we were about to do was going to be dangerous. The bully was an employer of several fourteen and fifteen-year-olds. They were being trained to become motel staff, maids, servers, butlers, maître d'hôtel, porters, etc. The course had cost their parents a small fortune, and was only offered once a year for three weeks in the school holidays. The candidates lived in a motel specially purchased for the training. Each participant would come away with a certificate, which would give them first in line standings for employment based around the course. Two years ago the original owner and trainer passed away from complications of influenza. The business had been sold, and this was the first year it was reopened. The new owner was and always had been a bully, ever since he could walk. He bullied kids in the park, and at his day care, so much that his parents were asked to remove him. He had become more of a bully the older he got. He had been expelled from several schools, and ended up having to finish school by distance, as no regular school would take him on. The trainees were only in their first week of the course, and already three had been thrown on to the bitumen car park, sustaining cuts and scratches. Two girls had been made into the sheets on a bed, so tightly they couldn't move, the door to the room had been locked and they had been left there for hours. If one of the other trainees tried to help them, they were knocked to the ground, and told to mind their own business. They had been starved, and had their knuckles whipped with a cane, yelled at, sworn at, verbally abused, ridiculed and threatened. At bed time all the doors were locked from the outside. They were given no privacy to use the bathroom, there was only one, and they all had to share it, and the door had been removed. A couple of the girls had taken to holding up sheets across the doorway, facing the road while others had their showers. Their punishment for this was they were made to strip down to their underwear and shower under the hose in the middle of the carpark. The new owner telling them he wasn't going to be responsible for girls getting into trouble with boys at his facility. All the trainees just wanted to go home, but one of the conditions of being there were no mobile phones, so they had no way of contacting home, and asking for help. A couple of them had tried running away to get help, but the new owner always caught them and dragged them back by their hair, and threw them into their rooms and locked the door. We were all disgusted at what was going on. It was going to be a long night as we had to do each rescue separately, there was only one teenager per room, and there were sixteen teens.

That was four each. It was almost sunrise by the time we had finished. Everyone was weary, and I was tempted to sleep on the beach for a couple of hours. Andy of course wouldn't have a bar of that. She sent Mishie and I off home, and flew off into the distance with the new GMF. I asked Mish to stay at mine and get some rest, but she said she had some stuff to get done at home. She could see I was physically and mentally wreaked, and refused to allow me to see her home first. She stopped at my place long enough to tuck me into bed. She then flew off into the night, promising to mind-speak to me her whole way home.

Except I must have fallen asleep and I awoke to her screaming out for me, in my mind. I was up and out of bed and in the air in a flash. Following the built-in radar I had where Mishie was concerned, I eventually found her, lying in a pool of mud at the edge of the river.

Chapter 28

"What the hell happened?" I asked her, "Are you hurt? Mishie, Mishie" I shook her, "Talk to me." She carefully sat up and she had blood dripping from a swelling bump on her head, her knee was banged up and her hand had been ripped open by oyster shells, that were on a rock beside her.

 "Andy **ANDY!**" I was screaming out in mind speak.

"We are on our way Joe, just a few more minutes," she assured me.

I ripped a piece of my shirt and stuck it onto her head where it was bleeding. Andy mind-spoke me, "Joe glitter it first, the glitter will help."

I did, and I glittered her knee and hand. I could see little pieces of oyster shell stuck in her hand. I gently tried to pull as much of it out as I could with my fingernails. "Mishie what the hell happened? Did you fall out of the sky?" I interrogated.

"I don't know, one minute I was flying along talking to your snoring self." Mishie was saying.

I blushed, "Yeah I'm so sorry Mishie, I must have nodded off."

She continued, "I was starting to descend, my house is just on the other side of the fence. Next thing I know something grabs my feet, and pulls me down. I tried to aim for the water, but it was all just so quick."

Just then Andy and the new fairy Alfie, landed on the grassy bank beside us. We used glitter and helped Mishie to get onto the grass. Andy checked her over and added more glitter to her wounds. I was looking around for some clues and I saw some weird sort of gooey stuff near the edge of the water where Mishie had fallen, it looked like green tadpole eggs. "What's this?" I asked Andy.

She came down to the water's edge to have a closer look, "Oh that's bad" she replied.

I raised my eyebrow at her, and at the same time Alfie exclaimed, "There is a mark around her ankles, like someone threw a rope around them and pulled it hard."

I jumped back up to Mishie, and sure enough she had rope burn around her ankles, but it wasn't normal rope burn, it had melted into her skin a little bit.

What the hell, I looked at Andy who was now standing beside me, holding a looped roll of rope loosely in her hand, "Found this in the sand," she said.

It has Osine acid on it, that's what has eaten the skin away. Andy reached down and glittered Mishie's ankles where the rope burn was. "Luckily it's not bad. It obviously it wasn't on there long enough to cause to much damage," she declared.

"Wait! What?" I ground out angrily, "An Osine attacked Mish? Well, where is it now? Coz I'm going to rip it apart with my bare hands." "Joe

watch your temper PLEASE," Andy begged. "I don't know where it is. It could be anywhere. My guess is that because Mishie tried to steer herself into the water, she would have dragged the Osine to the water's edge. Salt water hurts Osine, badly. That goo you found Joe, is the acid coating all Osine have on their bodies. It would have started to react to the salt water, and have been burning into the Osines skin. I think it has let go of the rope, and run away somewhere, either to get help or heal its self."

"How do I find it Andy?" I fumed.

"Joe", she cautioned me again. "Rosemary will be here any second, walk away, count to ten, or I will restrain you. If Rosemary hears you losing your temper, you're out, you know that."

I growled low in my throat and Alfie came over and grabbed my shoulder, "Let's go for a walk bro, Mishie is in perfectly capable hands. We won't go far just to the trees ok?" he commanded.

I allowed him to lead me away, just as Rosemary landed beside Andy on the grass. I watched from a distance as she glittered Mishie's wounds again. I saw her and Andy in deep mind-speak. Then she called to my mind, "Joe you have a deep red radius glowing all around you, are you going to be able to hold that temper of yours? Or am I going to have to restrain it for you?"

"You see my lifetime partner lying on the ground right? You can see she is hurt? You know it could have been worse?......................... " I spat out to her.

Alfie, interrupted mine and Rosemary's mind-speak and announced, "Sure he is going to control his temper, you just concentrate on fixing the sweet angel lying on the ground, and I will take care of this bad boy ok?"

With that he led me across the road, and down the block to an all-night petrol station, where we brought pastries and milks, then crossed the road and sat on a park bench overlooking the river stuffing our faces. "So, are you relaxed enough now to talk, or are you going to bite my head off as well?" Alfie shrugged.

"It's my fault she is hurt," I sighed. "All I do is hurt her. I can't even begin to tell you how much I want to protect her. My whole self-lives to please her, but somehow, I am forever messing it up. I should have flown her home. I wanted to, but she talked me out of it. I should never have let her. What if she had of been hurt worse? What if the Osine had of taken her? It would be all my fault." I cradled my head in my hands sobbing like a baby.

"It wasn't your fault. You didn't know what was going to happen. Do you blame Andy for it? Because maybe she should have flown with you both, seeing you both all the way home? Or maybe it was my fault? I'm the newbie, I am the one being babied at the moment, maybe it's my fault?" Alfie stated.

Just then the seat creaked and Mishie sat beside me hugging me, "It wasn't your fault Joe, it could just as easily have been anyone of us. But I am glad it was me, and that I live beside salt water. If it was any of you, you might not have made it."

Andy commented that Mishie was right it could have been anyone of us.

"Where's the almighty fairy mistress?" I enquired.

"She had to go," Andy muttered sighing. "Joe you really need to let it go, this thing with Rosemary has to stop."

I did not answer, but I threw up a few graphic pictures in her mind to remind her of all the things Rosemary had in my opinion, failed me on. In turn Andy threw into my mind a picture of a really badly beat up 4x4.

The sun was up, and I needed to get home and do chores. We walked Mishie to her door. I made her promise me she was ok, and I glittered her wounds, which in truth were all but gone now anyway. She hugged Andy and Alfie, getting a little too comfy, snuggled up to Alfie.

"Oi," I protested with a laugh, "That's my girl, and I don't share!" I really wasn't jealous, it was like some higher power had purposely brought us all together, and we were like one perfect unit, each fitting into our own little section, great as a single unit but unbeatable and spectacular together.

She let the others walk away a bit and grabbed me and hugged me until my insides almost burst, then she kissed my mouth, and turned my legs to jelly. "You need to be doing chores," she laughed pushing me away.

It took me a couple of minutes to walk comfortably, and another couple to catch up to the other two. As we were walking along the foreshore looking for a bus stop, out of the corner of my eye I saw something move from behind a line of trees. I didn't see what it was, but I had cold chills and instant goosebumps, without even realising what I was doing I sprinted off after it. I could hear Alfie yelling at me to stop. Then I could hear him trying to catch up to me. I sent an image to his mind of what I had seen, that was easier than trying to explain it. It had set off warnings throughout my mind and body, and I just knew it was the thing responsible for hurting Mishie. I wasn't gaining on it at first, and it was just a blur in the distance, but after about a kilometre of foreshore it started to slow down. I had started to gain distance, I could hear Alf panting about 400 metres behind me. I could also sense Andy close by.
"Be careful Joe," she ESP'd to me.
I was about fifty metres from it now, and I could clearly make out its features. It was hideous, snapping claw-like pincers on either hand, where it should have had a thumb and forefinger. It had a huge gut hanging over its denim cut off shorts, hanging down to its mid-thigh. It was wearing a three sizes too small green t-shirt, and it had on a pair of white joggers with the toes busted out of

them. Its huge feet sticking out through the hole, the shoes only covering about one half of the ugly feet. Small beady eyes on the side of its head near ears, that were shaped like a peanut, peered back at me. It reeked, bad, like throw up, and off sea food. Luckily, I didn't have time to stop and think about it. I was dry-retching and gaging, but I wasn't slowing down. I crash tackled it, leaping onto its back from three metres behind it. I tried to grab its hands to hold them behind its back, but they were covered in slime, and too slippery for me to hold. In an instant it had turned the tables, and thrown me over so it was on top of me, its knees digging into my thighs, its pinchers digging right into the soft flesh just below my collar bone. Blood was oozing from where they were sticking into me and the pain was almost unbearable. It pulled one of its claws free and punched me in the face, I heard my jaw bone crack.

It was laughing manically, "Say yes, say yes," it was repeating all most in a sing song tune over and over.

"Never," I screamed at it, suddenly feeling very weak. Then as suddenly as it began, the thing stopped and took off running away again. I felt a pair of strong arms slide under my arms and lift me to my feet, where I was face to face with Andy. "Joe," she sighed and blew glitter onto my face, my jaw snapping back into place as soon as the glitter hit my face. She held up her wrists and let glitter flow freely into the now bleeding profusely holes in my shoulders. "How is the pain?" she inquired, inspecting the damage now the bleeding was slowing.

"Bearable, I guess," I replied shrugging. The bleeding from my shoulders now just a slight trickle, and still slowing.

Just as Alfie caught up, "What the hell were you thinking? You could have been killed. You should have told me straight away, we are a team, you don't have to fight on your own anymore man. Hasn't the last little while taught you anything? I am HERE for you, you stubborn mule. You need to ask for help now. Stop and think about the rest of us for a change would ya!" he chastised me, at the same time as pulling me into a hug and patting my back, bro style.

I looked over his shoulder at Andy, she sighed again, "You could have been killed, how many times Joe, it is becoming a habit. I agree with everything Alfie just said. You need to stop and think things through or one day you are going to be killed or worse, be stripped of you glitter and wings. Your just lucky that Osine had just had a dip in salt water, and his poisonous slime had been diluted, or you would be wiggling round on the ground in excruciating pain, dying about now. It is very rare a G M F survives a direct hit to the veins from Osine toxin. As it is you're probably going to get very sick for a week or so, and won't be able to do anything."

I pushed myself away from Alfie, standing by myself, "I AM FINE," I ground out between my teeth, "Meanwhile that thing has got away. When are you all going to learn, I don't ask for any help. That thing nearly killed my girlfriend. What did you expect me to do?" I was starting to feel a little unsteady and wobbly on my feet and I felt Alf grab me just as my legs gave away. I sat on the ground for a good while, still feeling dizzy for what seemed like hours. Andy and Alfie were both hovering over me. At some point one of them provided water and food. After I had eaten, I started to feel a little better, and was soon able to stand. The sun was well and truly up now, so flying home wasn't going to be an option. Andy, happy with my progress, hugged me, and said she had to go, so we all headed to the main road to find a bus stop.

We found a bus stop, a kilometre or so further along the foreshore from where I had unsuccessfully attacked the Osine. The bus stop was a near a well-kept, neat and tidy amenities block.

Alfie and I waited on a Gold Coast bound bus. Andy winked at us and walked into the toilets, and never walked back out. But she did ESP us to please be careful. She told me that if I got any further symptoms or starting feeling worse to contact her immediately. She said she wouldn't be too far away, as she had some things to attend to in town, and would be staying close by for a few days. As we looked up, we saw tiny microscopic bits of glitter catching the sunlight as they fell from the sky.

I asked Alf where he lived and he said he was currently staying with some friends in the hinterlands, closer to the Southern Goldie, he shrugged and said he had some stuff to get together with his life, then he'd get a place of his own. I explained to him as best as I could, that him and I were going to be very close, and that he was now officially my brother from another mother. Nothing was ever going to come between us, and there was never EVER going to be anything he couldn't talk to me about, including the fact he had the hots for my girlfriend. He actually blushed and said, "So you can see that huh."

I Chuckled, and told him everybody could see that.

"I know she is yours, but a guy can dream. Someday I want what you have. I want someone to look at me like I am the gravity that is holding them upright on this planet," Alf declared.

It will happen I assured him and somehow I 100% knew it would. I told him there would ALWAYS be a bed for him at my place, if he ever needed it. I had a hunch he was going to need it sooner rather than later!

Chapter 29

When I finally got home, I wearily did my chores, thankful I had made dad install the automatic watering systems a while ago as I didn't think I would have been able to stand up and fill fifty water troughs. I think everything that had happened in the past few months was finally catching up with me, my body was starting to shut its self-down. I knew I would have to get some deep rest soon, or I was going to end up back in a hospital bed. I finished my chores and headed back to my room and laid on my bed staring at the ceiling going over the events of this morning. I understood now how Mishie had felt when I had the accident. The thought that I almost lost her to Osines this morning was making me feel sick. I kept reaching out to her in mind-speak, just to make sure she was still ok. My collar bone, where the thing stabbed me with its pinchers was aching a little, nothing I couldn't handle though. I had used some glitter on it earlier. My jaw was paining me a little so I had glittered that as well.

I Esp'd Andy about the Osine, she told me, no, rather commanded me, "To leave it alone." She said "It had fled, we didn't know to where yet. It would be dealt with, soon, but not by me, and not now!"

My eyes were getting heavier and soon I was snoring softly. I was having the most amazing dream. Kevin was standing beside Harry, in his stall in my stables and was smiling, whispering to Harry.

Harry was calm and Kevin jumped on his back and just sat there not moving. He looked like he was communicating via mind-speak with the big horse, the horse was nodding, and swayed his head a couple of times. Other than that, he was standing statue still. Occasionally Kevin would reach down and pat Harry's neck. Kevin then laid on the horses back and wrapped his arms around the stallion, and rubbed his face in his mane.

Then he slid off, and whispered, "My gift to you brother," he then turned to look directly at me, with a huge smile on his face. Then something startled me, and suddenly I was wide awake. It was just a dream I know, but there was something about it, it was somehow different to the other dreams I had had in my life. The image of Kevin standing, and sitting on Harry brought tears to my eyes, even though he never got to officially meet him, he was after all his horse. That's part of the reason I was trying so hard to make Harry well again, because he was Kevin's horse, and everything I had ever done with him was for Kevin. Harry's ribbons and trophies, all dedicated to my brother. I think the dream was a sign telling me that maybe he had moved on, and that he was happy now and I could stop fretting over him.

It was still dark outside, so I glittered myself back to sleep, I knew my body needed more time to recuperate.

 I woke to the sun shining through the glass door in my room.

Something about the air felt different today. It was like a fogginess had been lifted from me and I felt happier than I had done in a long time. I got dressed and headed out to do my chores. I was going to talk to dad in the next couple of days about hiring a saddle hand, whether he liked it or not, it had to happen. The stud was just too big for me to manage on my own now. We had over two hundred horses and foals at the present time. Most of the foals had already been purchased and were just waiting to be shipped out to their new owners as soon as they had been weaned.

Mostly, dad didn't come out to the paddocks or stables now, unless he was showing a horse buyer around. He spent a lot of time away on business trips all over the world, selling our horses, and their seed, for thousands of dollars. He was now paying aunt Denny to assist with the books and office duties.

I went around the paddocks feeding and checking on all the stock, watching foals jumping and prancing around, a few curious enough to come up and sniff me.

As I always I left my two special horses until last. Molly was getting a huge tummy now, the vet said she thought it might be twins. Another few weeks and we would know for sure. I would have to cut back on her showings soon, as I wouldn't get a girth to fit safety around her stomach.

Word had gotten out that she was expecting, and the offers for her foal had already started to come in. One overseas buyer had offered fifty million for the foal, unseen.

I fed her and brushed her down and sat with her in her pen, talking to her for an hour. I was watching Harry in the opposite pen and he was at his gate looking at me, whinnying, something he hadn't done since before the accident. I put it down to him wanting his food. I stood up and quietly made my way over to him so as not to spook him. He was pouring the ground softly with the tip of his hoof, just enough to make dust clouds. The closer I got to him the more he called out to me. Usually by the time I reached his gate, he would have turned and fleeted to the middle of his paddock, where he would watch me fill his trough then wait for me to move away before coming to eat. Not today. Today he stood at the gate. When I got to him, I tentatively reached up to pat his muzzle, expecting him to rare and shie away. He didn't move and he let me pat him, and even pushed his nose into my hand. I reached up and patted his neck, being mind-full of his body language, and ready to jump out of his way if he became agitated, but he just stood there. I chanced going into his pen and reached up and patted his massive shoulder. He turned his head towards me, every muscle in my body stiffened. I willed myself to relax and just breathe. His eyes were huge and calm no signs of him rolling them and he reached his muzzle to my back and rubbed it against me.

He stretched his neck around further and wrapped his head around my waist and pulled me close to him, like Molly does.

He held me there for several minutes with his eyes closed, just cuddled into me. I was crying. My big stallion was finally coming round, he nuzzled his head under my butt trying to push me up onto his back. I gingerly grabbed a handful of his mane and swung myself up onto his back, immediately clenching my legs, just in case. He shook his big head, but just stood there. I looked across at Molly who was watching the whole thing from her pen and she neighed softly. As I flicked my eyes back to Harry, I saw a flash of light out of the corner of my eye, and heard a voice in my head, "I will always love you little brother."

The end

a

Authors note

Bullying is NEVER ok.

You're not stupid, or weak, or ugly, or someone's punching bag, and your definitely not here for some sickos sexual gratification.

You are amazing, and you can stand up for yourself, even if that means asking for help.

The definition of bullying is this: Bullying is an ongoing and deliberate misuse of power in relationships through repeated verbal, physical and/or social behaviour that intends to cause physical, social and/or psychological harm. It can involve an individual or a group misusing their power, or perceived power, over one or more persons who feel unable to stop it from happening.

There are six main types of bullying, and they are:

Physical, this includes any form of another person touching you with intent to hurt you. Kicking, punching, pinching, hair pulling, shoving, pushing, tripping you, slapping, or hitting your person with another object, such as a bat or stick.

Verbal bullying, yes words can hurt, they can make us feel ashamed of everything we are. This includes derogatory comments, teasing, tormenting, name calling, put downs, and being repeatedly laughed, or made fun of.

Cyberbullying, let's face it most of us practically live on line, Facebook, twitter, or any other social media sites, and chat groups are our go-to to contact our family members that don't live at home anymore, it's where we connect with our friends. But unfortunately it's also the way cyberbullies and trolls get to us. In an ideal world, we would shrug off keyboard warriors and see them for what they are. NOBODIES. But unfortunately sometimes what they post online about us can really have a negative impact on our well being and mental state.

Cyberbullying is when someone uses the internet to share hurtful comments, photos taken out of context, slander, embarrass, threaten, harass or otherwise harm someone else. If the event takes place with an adult present, the term changes to cyber-harassment. It can also be called cyberstalking.

Some examples of cyberbullying are, posting hurtful comments, sharing hurtful or embarrassing images, actual photographs, cartoon depictions, drawings etc.

Making threats online. Trying to bribe you by saying if you don't do want they will hurt a family member, best friend etc.

Sending hurtful emails or text messages.

Emotional Bullying, this differs slightly from verbal bullying, although it can be included here as well.

Emotional bullying is when your peers don't include you in activities, pick you always last for the soccer team, that kind of thing. It's when your friends try to steal your limelight, you may have finished a project with a class mate, and most of the effort was yours, but they brag that they did it all, and you did nothing. Your friends' group might be going to the movies, and they invite everyone else but you. This is emotional bullying, and it hurts. Some ways an emotion bully might hit their target are, spreading lies and rumours about you. An ex-best friend might tell everyone things you told them in confidence. Things that you are embarrassed about, like the time you didn't quite make it to the toilet in time, Or about family breakdowns, or other personal family goings on.

They may try to tell your other friends to keep away from you, and use tactics like bribery to isolate you from others, saying things like, if you be their friend, not yours they will buy others lunch etc.

When someone deliberately breaks your trust over and over, that is emotional bullying as well.

Prejudicial Bullying, being bullied because of your skin colour, religion, personal beliefs, hair colour/style, your social status, what you eat, how much money you/ your family have/make, where you live, your sexual orientation, your choice of sport, what you watch on tv, what you read. The list for this one goes on and on. It's not ok to bully anyone for their personal choices. Actually it's not

d

even any of anyone else's business, and it certainly does not make you any less of a person/friend/classmate/team mate/ partner, etc.

Sexual bullying, can take many forms. Any form of sexual acts that do not have full consent from both parties. Including forcing someone to have sexual intercourse with you. Forcing someone to preform sexual acts to you. Forcing someone to accept sexual acts from you. These things are also illegal, and are called sexual assault, the person doing these things know they are doing wrong,

so they try to scare you into doing what they want by threatening to hurt people you care about.

THEY are lying, they don't want to get in trouble for their acts. If you or someone you know is being forced against their will to participate in sexual acts, IT'S not ok. It's not your fault. Please talk to someone you trust, and seek help.

Sexual bullying is also, sending someone obscene pictures, exposing yourself to someone, inappropriately touching someone, continuously commenting on the changes puberty is having on someone's body, or trying to shame that person because of the speed, or lack of development.

Exposing someone's sexual preferences before they are ready to do it themselves, and making fun of them, or trying to change their minds. Spreading gossip about a girls promiscuity, regardless of if it's true or not.

e

This kind of bullying is mostly girl orientated, but boys can be just as mean and insensitive.

If you have been in a relationship with someone, and the relationship has ended, IT'S NOT ok to share any aspects of that relationship with anyone else, this includes any sexting messages.

While these books are totally fictitious, Bullying is not, it's real and it affects everyone.

If your being bullied in ANYWAY, please I beg you to talk to someone you trust, someone who can help you. If you are too scared to talk to someone because you think it's happening because you deserve it, or because you're a bad person, or whatever reason, I promise you that isn't true. You might not think so, but there are a lot of people who care about you, and want to protect you. It's not shameful to ask for help, we all need some help at some point.

PLEASE PLEASE ask someone for help.

Some of the information on these pages has been sourced from thebullyshield.com

f

Kids Helpline https://kidshelpline.com.au/
Anytime. Any reason.

Phone 1800 55 1800

Beyond blue

Beyond Blue is an independent, not-for-profit
organisation working to reduce the impact of
anxiety, depression and suicide in Australia.
www.beyondblue.org.au/who-does-it-
affect/youngpeople

Phone 1300 22 4636

Glitter Magic Fairies

Like and follow our Facebook page to get updates on when new books in the series will be released, and all things G M F related!

Just search Glitter Magic Fairies.

h

Glitter Magic Fairies

Mishie

Mishie and Carly are the best sisters ever, they share everything. Until Carly goes away to another state for dance school, and Mishie starts to hear a voice in her head from a two-hundred-year-old women.

k

www.ingramcontent.com/pod-product-compliance
Lightning Source LLC
Chambersburg PA
CBHW020515120726
47904CB00003B/848